A Messa

Dedicated to all those whose lives were

changed irrevocably

by Hurricane Katrina in August 2005.

Jacqueline Swann

CONTENTS

Author's Preface   6

1   A Day in the Life   9

2   Honey, I sold the farm   18

3   Paranoid Pessimists or Prophets   21

4   Families Make our Lives   38

5   Religious Visionary or Crazy?   60

6   Exodus on a Sunday   70

7   The Big Break   81

8   Dreams Come True   93

9   Clay Feet   103

10   A Dance with the Devil   116

11   Don't Blame Me   130

12   Fear Always Triumphs   138

13   Refuge or Jail?   143

14   Good-bye to New Orleans   150

15   Interregnum   155

A Message from Katrina

16 Stand Down   166

17 Ambition, Thou Fiend   199

18 Reporting It Doesn't   211
    Fix It

19 Resettling America   226
    Series

20 Shrinking the Footprint   250

21 Epilogue: Riding the   259
    Camel

    Notes   280

    Works of Interest   282

    The New Earth Song   284

    Acknowledgements   288

    About the Author   289

Author's Preface

When Hurricane Katrina crashed into New Orleans on August 29, 2005 I saw a tipping point event occurring. An acceptance of the reality of global warming (now referred to as climate change) was pushed into the minds of many North Americans. The last thirteen years have given more and more details to the future I glimpsed during Hurricane Katrina. Sadly, the events of the last decade have not changed its direction. Nor has the catastrophic devastation of each storm or wild fire inspired enough of us to change our choices.

For several months after Hurricanes Katrina and Rita I awoke at night with scenes for a novel keeping me from sleep. I had inspirational bouts of writing, but life got in the way. Retirement, gardening, grandkids, editing the novel with friends, all ate up the years. Maybe I was waiting for Drew Dellinger's poem fragment from 'hieroglyphic stairway'*. I first read it in Ian Angus' book, 'facing the anthropocene (fossil capitalism and the crisis of the earth system)'. I share it here with you.

it's 3:23 in the morning
and I'm awake
because my great great grandchildren
won't let me sleep
my great great grandchildren

A Message from Katrina

ask me in dreams
what did you do while the planet was plundered?
what did you do when the earth was unraveling?

surely you did something
when the seasons started failing?

as the mammals, reptiles, birds were all dying?

did you fill the streets with protest
when democracy was stolen?

what did you do
once
you
knew?

Well, I started writing this novel. I hope you enjoy it. I hope it helps you decide what you'll do.

Jacqueline Swann

CHAPTER 1

A DAY IN THE LIFE

New Orleans,

August 2005

"Coli", yelled George. She heard him shambling his way down the hall. His head bent to clear the doorway. His football player's shoulders and torso blocked the light, throwing a shadow across Coli's computer and desk. She looked up to see her boss, sparse blonde-grey hair shiny with sweat, tie undone and hanging limply across his blue sweat-moist shirt. Sweat dripped from his bushy eyebrows.

"Have to get the AC fixed," he huffed. "You look as hot as I feel. I thought you were born and bred here, used to it."

"No one ever gets used to it. Besides, I was spoiled by four years away at Northeastern U. doing broadcast journalism. I loved those crisp Springs and Falls," said Coli.

"As a trade-in on today they'd be good."

"But the winters? Whoa! Nobody told me that the fluffy white stuff was so bloody cold! And that there were months of it. Pretty ugly by spring, great piles of melting grey and brown sludge."

"Try playing football in Minnesota with the North Wind from the Canadian Prairies slicing through your bones."

"Poor George. Good thing your wife insisted on retiring to a No Winter Zone."

George peered at her computer screen. She saw him change from Dad figure to boss. "How you doin' with the program on yesterday's jury meeting? Ready to air yet?

"I'm just editing it now. I've removed most of the pencil tapping, but I'm still working on shuffled papers and pregnant pauses. It's the usual mix of how to keep the streets welcoming to tourists, the drug deals off the main drag, a close watch on minor criminals and their big brothers." Coli looked up at George's rather large nose and added, "And that preacher, ah, Reverend Weekes was on about re-enforcing or rebuilding the levees."

"Did you get statements from each of the main players?"

"Yup, I looked cute and willing to be impressed."

"Will it fit the time space?"

"Probably it'll be a little short."

"All right, put in a couple of extra ads if you need to. If that's still not enough, put in an informational inset. Maybe call it: 'Your Local Government And You'.

"Can I do a voice over and ghost background of myself?"

"Okay, but watch that 'vaulting ambition which o'er-leaps itself.' "*

George turned around to leave and then checked himself. "Don't forget. You're covering that weather conference "Emerging Weather Trends" at the Grand Hotel.

Coli attacked the stuff on her desk with hope. She finally found the brochure under her coffee cup. A blob of dried coffee had blotted out part of the hotel's name. "Wow! I never had any reason to sashay into that fancy lobby before."

"Well," George eyed up Coli's cut-offs and flip-flops. "Wear a nice suit. You'll be representing Easy Times Cable Station."

"Sure, I've got a navy blue one. I'll be the perfect picture of professional poise. Wow! The Grand Hotel. The first rung of my ladder to success."

George shook his head. "Don't be too excited. On what you get paid, you certainly couldn't spend the night there."

"Not yet maybe, but some day."

George turned away again. "Remember, 'vaulting ambition which o'er-leaps itself'."

"Shakespeare freak," she tossed down the hall behind him.

Two hours later she had read the folder and edited the jury meeting program. It was now ready to air on the *Easy Times* local cable news program, *About Town*. She was late to leave work, again. She was starving and her fridge contained only the remains of her least favourite yogurt. She rifled through her purse and found her emergency money hidden in the corner pocket. The need for a decent meal had reached emergency status for her.

The bus ride home to the French Quarter was hotter and slower than usual. Coli stepped off the bus and decided to change her routine. Instead of turning left to her apartment, she turned right and headed for her old waitressing job. She had been promising herself for far too long that she would go by to say 'hi'.

The street hadn't changed much in her time away. The same small, brightly painted shops and houses were there. Each one was a little smack of colour: rose, yellow, sky blue and orange. She saw it all: the pots of plants and flowers near doors and private entrances, the wrought iron rusting slightly from its former glory. The restaurant sign, *The Crawfish*, still needed some fresh paint. The tiny, local restaurant was tucked into a back street but the food was all soul and more to the point, pretty cheap. It all seemed remarkably the same in comparison with how much she felt she had changed. She waved at Jolene who was waiting at one of the few tables that was still occupied so late in the evening.

Coli flopped down at her favourite table behind the indoor palm. Mama Alphonse had been told of her arrival and shuffled over to her table. She was short, solid and vibrantly alive. She said, "Where y'at?"

"Mama Alphonse, y'all lookin' good," said Coli, smiling in her soul. She remembered when she was a miserable teenager feuding with her own mama. She remembered all the times that Mama Alphonse had helped her, and later hired her as a waitress. Coli was caught in Mama Alphonse's massive hug. She was surprised by how much she enjoyed it and wished her own mother were given to hugs. She returned the gesture with love. "I can actually be a customer tonight but I can only afford $10."

"Don't worry, I got you' favourites, Honey Chil'," Mama Alphonse chuckled. She ambled back to the kitchen and returned shortly, bringing a steaming dish with her.

Coli smelled the spicy aroma of her jambalaya and ate it with unfeigned joy as she listened to Mama Alphonse give her the news of the parish. Then, Mama Alphonse talked of her grown daughters, Louisa and Hélène, and their numerous children.

"You bin to see my great-nephew Orlando? He workin' in that travel agency on Charles Street durin' the day and playin' jazz with his band over at that nightclub, the River Daze, some nights."

Coli searched her tired brain and vaguely remembered Orlando. He had been a senior when she was just a junior. He was one of several guys she had nodded to but never really had the nerve to smile at. She said, "I haven't heard him yet but one night when I'm not so tired I'll try to go by."

"You don't be no stranger now you back in town, Collette," said Mama Alphonse as she walked Coli back to the door.

Coli carefully unlocked the door to her tiny apartment in the French Quarter. She loved its strange corners and all that old brick and wrought iron on her tiny balcony. It had been an important part of her plans for her future. Her own place, quiet and tidy, where she didn't have to worry about what state her mother was in. She felt relaxed and welcomed until she noticed that the light for her phone messages was winking at her in the gloom of her desk in the corner.

A Message from Katrina

She pressed the button gingerly. "Where the fuck are you?" screamed her drunken mother's voice. "You think you can ignore me, Collette Dunk, and pretend to be Coli Duncan, cable TV's greatest reporter? I seen more of you behind that silly In-for-ma-tion-al fucking inset on *About Town* than I seen of you in the flesh. Now you're too fancy to come and see me," her mother screamed into the phone before slamming it down.

I can't deal with this, thought Coli in despair, before she fell back onto her bed. She lay there knowing that calling her mama right now wouldn't lead to an acceptable conversation for either of them. Her old anger was rising one more time. She realized that she was rhythmically smashing her right fist into the palm of her other hand. Not again, she thought. Ever since her first memory, she had felt her mother's bitterness reaching out at her. It was as if her mother blamed her for existing. As if she destroyed something her mother valued by being in the same room.

As a child she had tried being good, but her mother took that for granted. Being obnoxious brought the back of her mother's hand on the nearest part of her body. No change in her behaviour moved her mother from her reluctant care for her child. Coli only vaguely remembered her father. When she asked her mother about him, she was met with silence or the sound of the sip of one more mouthful of Abita from one more go cup. Finally, she learned to avoid any mention of her father and a fragile truce had bloomed between them.

The truce was, however, very fragile and Coli tried to keep her anger and disappointment with her mother tamped down hard. So, she couldn't phone tonight. She was too angry and her mother was too drunk. She stared at her hands and tried to force them to stop moving.

Action, that's what I need. She bounded off her bed and stormed to her tiny bathroom. She slammed the door and felt a bit better. She reached for her hairbrush and stared into the mirror. Yup, she looked just like her mother, dark long hair awry and anger marring her face. Fine bones from her French ancestors and sun kissed skin from her Cajun ones. At least she was taller than her petite mother and had more flesh on her bones. Her mother was the angular shape of a person who would rather drink than eat. Well, she would not be that woman.

Coli raked the tangles out of her hair. Her straight shining hair made her feel better. She brushed her teeth so hard she could almost see the enamel rubbing off and felt a bit better. She peeled off her sweaty clothes and pulled on one of her over-size t-shirts to sleep in. She dumped her clothes in the hamper and stomped out of the bathroom.

Coli started pacing the small living room. Around and around the coffee table and the chair she paced and muttered, muttered and paced. "Not fair, not fair, not fair!"

She didn't know how long she went round and round but finally her anger ground down. She was exhausted but knew that she would make it through this episode, too. She did feel a bit better.

Maybe tomorrow, Coli thought. Yeah, I'll phone Mama tomorrow she promised herself. She looked at her hands and carefully relaxed them, one more time. She lay down and shut her eyes tightly, trying to will herself to sleep. She had work tomorrow and had to get up far too early.

CHAPTER 2

HONEY, I SOLD THE FARM

Marilyn usually liked this time after school. She could drive home slowly, noticing the nice growth of soybeans in vibrant green rows. She could relish her short commute from Grand Falls to the farm. Today had been a crazy day at school, a Wednesday and a full moon. She was so tired that she could barely turn into the driveway. At least my planning is done for tomorrow, she thought. It sure gets harder after fifty-five to make it through the day. Thank the Lord, she had that leftover gumbo for supper. Now, what to go with it? Her mind just refused to work.

She slowly levered herself out of the car, regretting those extra forty pounds she didn't need. She gathered her books and papers from the back seat and headed inside by the kitchen door. The smells of okra and chicken wafted towards her as she opened the door. Strange. Was that Walter in front of the sink? Stranger and stranger.

A Message from Katrina

"Hi, Marilyn honey. It was getting later and later so I thought you might like some help with supper. I made a salad and brought up a bottle of last years' wine."

"Wine? Are we celebrating something? I'm so tired I might fall asleep before we get started."

"Yup, I sold the farm today!'

"You mean to that basketball player with all that money? That Jubal Weekes who used to spend his summers over at Tom's, helping with the hogs?"

"Yup"

"Thank God. Maybe now I can retire and go live in a new condo without a leaky roof or a sagging porch."

"Well, that might be a bit different than you thought."

"If it involves living in an RV trailer, you can sign the divorce papers after I've finished this wine."

"No, I've changed my mind about the trip to the Great Lakes. There might be more exciting stuff happening right here."

"Here, in Grand Falls? That'll be the day. This town has been dying for thirty years. All the family farms have been failing or just getting by."

"Now, Marilyn honey, we bin doin' okay."

"Well, Walter honey, we do still seem to spend all my wages too."

"Let's eat and then I'll tell you all about it." Walter was trying hard to keep Marilyn interested. "You know that Reverend Weekes who's been a guest pastor down at the Baptist Church? It's his son who's the basketball player with all the money to buy our place. He wants to run an organic farm, and build some condos to house people who want to relocate from New Orleans."

"That'll be the day, city folks returning to the country."

"There's more to it than that. He wants to rebuild the community. He's talking about a recycling plant in the old tobacco warehouse to grind up sneakers to make walkways and cycling paths all over the country. But more than that, he asked me if we wanted to be part of it. You know, buy one of his condos and help him start the farm production. I could be a consultant," he finished with wry humour.

"This is all too much for me today, Walter. Let me think about this with my feet up."

CHAPTER 3

PARANOID PESSIMISTS OR PROPHETS?

Coli staggered off the bus, clutching her mini-cam and back-up cassette. " I live for the day the station can afford my assistant and state-of-the-art equipment," she muttered to herself.

Just then she looked up at the Grand Hotel. The renovations for the Conference Center had been done quite tastefully in the style of the hotel's original architecture. This historic hotel in the French Quarter had white neo-Greek columns supporting second floor balconies. Four large Spanish Oaks towered over the main entrance. Coli thought fondly of 'Gone with the Wind' whenever she saw them. The Conference Center was off to the north side of the main building but repeated the large columns that hid the car park below. The main floor repeated the black curling railings on the terraces outside the main conference halls.

Coli started up the stairs with enthusiasm. Finally, she had a good reason to walk through that magnificent lobby! She tried hard not to loiter and gawk as she headed for the Conference Center. The coffee tables were edged with gold and the brocaded chairs carried through with a dark red and gold paisley design. She hoped that her lightweight navy blue suit lived up to the surroundings.

Her sleeveless, white, cotton blouse seemed to help absorb her sweat. No, she thought to herself, her perspiration. Southern women did not sweat. Although she had lived in this drained swamp at the edge of an ocean most of her life, the damp suffocating heat of August surprised her every year. No wonder the number of tourists dropped even more in August.

Thinking of tourists led her to thoughts of Mama Alphonse and her great-nephew Orlando. She wondered if he found it hard to spend his days charming would-be tourists to visit the Big Easy and then changing into a musician by night. That thought led her to think about what Orlando might really be like and why Mama Alphonse had made a point of mentioning him last night. She promised herself that she would go to *The River Daze* when she had the time and the money, just to see.

She was so deep in her thoughts that she walked into a rope. She stopped suddenly and looked up to see a thick, soft cord, looping from stanchion to stanchion in front of the conference rooms.

Trying to recover gracefully, she located exactly where she needed to enter. Outside the main doors, she took great pride in flashing her station affiliation badge at the doorman. Then, she walked purposefully toward the media section.

First of all, she assembled her camera and stand. She aligned it carefully to take in the speaker's podium and the screen behind. She settled herself down to learn as much as she could. She needed to figure out how to present the relevant bits so that she still had a viewing public at the end of her show.

The first speaker, Mr. C. Merriman, started to present his topic, *'The Cyclical Nature of Hurricane Patterns'*. She shifted in her chair as her rear began to feel numb. She quietly stood up and checked her camera angle. The speakers and data started to merge together after a while.

She could feel herself perspiring even in the supposedly air-conditioned conference room. Maybe it was all those graphs, charts and just plain spooky bits of information. She would need to choose carefully with editing her tape. Sure, she knew that parts of Florida had been evacuated four times last year and that there had been millions in property damage but even in paradise there had been a snake, right?

She and her mama had been hunkered down more than once as another hurricane blew in from the Gulf. She quickly blocked the frightening images of a small child cocooned in blankets in the tub in the "safest" room while the wind howled and the whole trailer shook with the gusts. The hurricanes hadn't stopped just because she'd grown up. Hurricane Cindy had already crashed ashore in early July this year and reminded everyone, with flooding and blackouts, that they did indeed live in hurricane alley.

It looked like this section was just wrapping up. She needed to stretch, visit the washroom, and try to pinpoint the speakers she wanted to interview later.

Coli had targeted her hopefuls for interviews at the next break. She put a new tape into her camera and settled into her chair again with renewed enthusiasm, but asked herself if the cable television audience had as much interest in the weather as her boss seemed to have. She peered at the next speaker, a tall, African American, with close-cropped curly hair. His handsome face seemed vaguely familiar. She looked up at the screen for his power point presentation. The title was '*Extreme Weather: Get Ready for the Big One*'. He was showing a chilling slide show of past hurricanes and the damage that they had caused. She watched with panic rising in her. You're an adult now, she reminded herself. These are only photos. She took a couple of deep breaths and settled in to pay attention.

Jordan Weekes looked up at his audience and started to speak in a deep, authoritative voice. "Most of us here have lived through more than one hurricane. * We all have stories about Audrey or Ethel, Betsy, Camille, Andrew or Ivan. We've all heard of roofs left two streets away on top of the preacher's prize azaleas. Here his voice held a slight twinkle. We've all seen uprooted trees and the scattered debris of our personal treasures. We are all made uneasy by stories of families in attics with an axe and no alternative but to chop their way out to the roof. These storms are bad enough but the situation of our city makes the results of extreme weather events even more profound.

"This is not new knowledge to most of you. Let me just give a short summary of how we have ended up where we are now. There have always been storms and flooding here." He turned to his power point slide showing a very old map of the local coastline. "In 1718, when the first French colonists settled along the crescent-shaped bend of the Mississippi River, heavy rains sent floodwaters roaring through their humble homes. So, why did they stay?

They, like us, couldn't overlook the trade advantages of a settlement where the third largest river in the world and ocean shipping meet. This trade advantage sent them to making rudimentary dikes, no more than three feet high around their new town. Next year, when the flood came again, they rejected nature's message. They made the dikes higher and brought in dirt to create higher land where they needed it. The next year they once again rejected the river's message and built the dykes higher. Have we learned anything yet from nature? No, we still believe that commerce and profit trump nature's messages.

"This same process has gone on for three hundred years until we now see dykes higher than three story buildings. We are proud of our human commerce and constructions. We showcase our courage and hope through our skyscrapers, heritage homes, towering levees, pumps, spillways, locks, and jetties. Unfortunately, most of our courage and hope has been devoted to fighting against nature instead of supporting or even hearing its messages.

"All of our ingenious construction may not be enough to sustain our commerce or our city. There are three more factors which may cause disaster all around us. Many of you have heard the term, 'global warming', and various estimates of how much sea levels may rise and when. The previous speaker showed the details and reasons for several different scenarios. For a city already below sea level, any rise of sea level will be costly and threatening."

Jordan Weekes turned to his glass of water and took a long swig. Coli realized that she was parched as well and fumbled in her bag for her water. She could feel her pulse racing a bit with unease. She hadn't anticipated that a weather conference would be so unnerving. She turned her attention to the speaker again, just as he raised his eyes to the audience and gave them more bad news.

"Our second major problem is land subsidence. This is a natural occurrence at the mouth of any river. As you know, all rivers deposit alluvial soils where the river meets the tides. This soil is very fine and silty, and naturally unstable. Over time, the water of the bottom layers is squeezed out and the embedded organic matter decomposes. Thus, the soil naturally shrinks and compacts itself. As I am speaking, all of southern Louisiana is sinking, sinking, sinking." Jordan Weekes stopped and looked at his audience. He let the magnitude of this natural process assault them.

"In the twentieth century alone, the land here has subsided about two feet." He raised his head again and took in his silent audience. "By now, you may wonder why we still have a city here. Thus, we arrive at our third major factor: the soil carried down the mighty Mississippi and deposited at its mouth, creating acres and acres of swamps and islands stretching far out into the gulf.

"When Jean Baptiste Le Moyne, sieur de Bienville, landed in 1718 at the site that would become Nouveau Orleans, the coast of Louisiana looked nothing at all like it does today. The land between that original settlement and the Gulf of Mexico featured dark, dense tracts of forests.

"Heading toward the sea, these forests became freshwater marshes and swamps full of spartina grass and water loving trees. Then, as salt levels rose the trees diminished and the swamps became full of flocks and flocks of birds."

Wow, thought Coli, I really should get out more. I wonder if Mama Alphonse's great-nephew Orlando's travel agency has any tours. That I could afford she added to herself. Then she tuned back into the presenter.

"Finally, reaching the edge of the Gulf of Mexico, was a network of tall and broad barrier islands. These islands were nature's protective walls set stubbornly against the powerful Gulf. Some, like Isles Dernieres, were twenty to thirty miles long and did, for a time, support human communities with hotels and homes as well as breeding grounds for pelicans and terns.

"This is what coastal Louisiana looked like on the maps of the early explorers and state cartographers in the 1700s and 1800s." He showed a map of a coastline very different from the one Coli knew.

"Even as late as 1916, the jungle-like forests southwest of New Orleans, made a convincing backdrop for the very first Tarzan movie.*

A Message from Katrina

"When I first began exploring this very same coast as a new husband, visiting my wife's Cajun family, almost everything I just described was gone. So was most of the economy based on tourism, fishing, trapping and alligator hunting. Only a small and very skilled group of Cajuns and Vietnamese immigrants remain.

"So where have all the swamps and barrier islands gone? Why do we now have open water in the Gulf and the tattered remains of an ever-shrinking coastline? Yes, we do have that normal subsidence of the land near the river delta. However, in the previous centuries there was actually a net growth of land in the delta. Yes, a net growth! Why? Remember all that silt and soil brought down by the river? In its normal, slow, meandering flow to the gulf, the river dropped its sediment to the bottom, building banks, swamps and islands.

That all changed three hundred years ago when dikes, levees, channels and most spectacularly, in the last few decades, the Go Canal, redirected and spurted out the river and its soils. The flow is so successfully channelled that the sediment is presently falling over the edge of the continental shelf into deep waters where it may take a millennia for the soils to reach the surface of the gulf as islands.

"So, we are here today at a weather conference knowing that we have ignored nature's messages about the balance between land subsistence and land building at the mouths of rivers. We also know that we will have more hurricanes and storms, only now, there are almost no barrier islands to slow down winds and buffer the city which is still sinking. Not only that, if the hurricane arrives at the right angle it could slam right up our largest canals and hurl a body punch at the heart of our city and our lives." With that dramatic announcement, Jordan Weekes glared at his audience and abruptly sat down.

The ensuing silence broke Coli's attention. She had been sort of aware of some of his points but had never added them up to realize how vulnerable the city was, especially in low lying areas, like in the Ninth Ward, where her mama's trailer was. She shifted her sore rear in her power suit and decided she'd better get back to work. She'd try to get a few interviews on tape. She hustled herself over behind the speakers' table. Carefully balancing her camera on her shoulder she approached the first of her targeted interviewees.

"Excuse me, Mr. Merriman. Could you please summarize the main part of your theory for the viewers of *Easy Times Cable TV*?" She shifted her camera towards him.

"Yes, Ms Duncan," he said, squinting at her media badge, which she had proudly held up at eye-level. "Although some people seem to think that we have had an unprecedented number of hurricanes and tropical storms just lately, there is data to show major storms do tend to cluster in 25 to 40 year cycles."

"So you don't subscribe to the theory that global warming is causing an increase in these events."

"If you remember my presentation of the storm data from 1935 to the present, you will remember that we have had some major storms long before any theories of global warming were tossed about." Coli became aware that a tall dark man with a subdued Afro was glaring at them from behind Mr. Merriman's shoulder. Coli realized that he was the last speaker. She squinted her eyes to catch the corner of his name tag. It read ….st Weather Data Collection and underneath …dan Weekes.

"Mr. Weekes, you look as if you don't agree with Mr. Merriman's conclusions," said Coli, as she watched Merriman turn his head with a glacial frown as he saw who was behind him.

"With respect to Mr. Merriman", replied Weekes, " I know that during the last four years, the frequency and strength of hurricanes and tropical storms have increased every year which is considerably longer and stronger than any previous cluster in Mr. Merriman's historical data." By now both men were glaring at each other and Coli could feel the air around her start to vibrate.

"Thank you very much for your views", she said with a nervous smile. "This is Coli Duncan of *Easy Times Cable TV* from the Grand Hotel where the *Conference on Emerging Weather Trends* is unfolding this weekend.

She couldn't pack up her gear fast enough. She shoved it as quickly as she could into her packs, turned around and ran right into a mountain of flesh in a tastefully dark suit. Large hands gripped her and a familiar voice said, "Ms Duncan, imagine running into you here." As he put her back on her feet, Coli thought, Reverend Weekes and Weekes the climatologist, that's why he'd looked familiar, a father and son combo. She smiled weakly again and thought that she was beginning to know how damsels in distress must have felt.

"Some of these theories are pretty hard to take: especially the melting ice caps, disappearing glaciers, subsiding continental shelves and vanishing barrier islands. My parishioners in the Ninth Ward are going to need those levees repaired with even more speed than I thought."

Jordan Weekes, who was standing slightly behind his father couldn't stop himself from rolling his eyes as his father once again jumped on his hobbyhorse. Ms Duncan was turning away from them and he knew he couldn't let this opportunity slip past him. He called to her, "Ms Duncan, I'd like to leave you my card. My wife, Lucille, is a member of the *Restore Coastal Louisiana Now* group, and she would very much like to talk to you about a local program on their issues." He smiled at Coli as he handed over his card.

Walter was starting to get a little annoyed with Jubal. His voice came through the phone with a whining note. "It's just not going to work if I can't get any help with the accounts."

"I thought you said everything on the farm was going pretty good now you have Enrico Mendez to help you with the planting and getting together a team of reliable pickers," replied Jubal.

"Yeah, that's working out good but it's keeping track of the money and the wages and all the damn regulations. Seems to be more every day. Changing to organic farming is bringing the suits out of their offices to see if our farm really is doing what we say we're doing. Nobody cared when I was following those pesticide spray programs and buying the right fertilizers."

"You said there'd be a 'period of adjustment'", returned Jubal with more patience than he felt.

"You said this would be a part-time consultant job that would fit in good with retirement. If I had an accountant manager type working with me it would be.

Marilyn said just the other day that she saw more of me before I sold the farm and got myself semi-retired."

"Walter, all this money you're spending has to be made. I'm on the road for a run of three basketball games and then maybe I can come down and we can work something out."

"Why don't we do it now?"

"I'm already late for a family dinner and I've got to go. I'll see you at the start of next week." Jubal hung up the phone with relief. What a dumb idea to think that he could run a farm.

Walter chuckled after he hung up. "Used you as an excuse there, Marilyn."

"Not the first time," she replied dryly as she closed the last math workbook she had needed to correct for the next day.

"That boy don't know as much as he needs to."

"He'll get there if you keep asking him the right questions. Besides he used to work for his uncle, Tom Weekes, at Pineridge Farm during the summers when he was in school. Old Tom is one of the few farmers around here that isn't always in at the bank to start his new season."

"I wouldn't be in at the bank neither if he'd just get me an accountant," grumbled Walter.

A Message from Katrina

As Coli edited and polished her *About Town, Weather is Us* report, she thought about Reverend Weekes. He sure seemed to be fixated on the levees issue. She wondered when he had time to minister to his church. Oh well, even her mother attended his services when she was sober enough and she, herself, had been dragged along often enough in her childhood. He may have been muttering about levees then too.

When Coli finally finished it was late again. She was tired but needed something more. Maybe it was time to listen to Orlando's music. She had to prove to herself that she was not a hopeless workaholic, as bad as her mother, just in a different way. She looked at her watch. Good, just enough time to catch a taxi to River Daze, slowly sip one beer, and hear 'my grand-nephew Orlando'.

Of course, the place was small, crowded and very mellow. The music was jazz as only New Orleans does it, sinking into its listeners, body and soul. Coli nursed one beer and floated with the sound. She tried to pick out Orlando and had it narrowed down to two guys, both in their twenties. Both interesting examples of how a blending of First Nations, Spanish, French and African bloodlines had produced shades from ivory to café-au-lait in its descendants.

She really didn't know which one, until the set ended. Then, the lighter skinned, muscular musician started to wind between tables, talking to friends and fans but always heading slowly in her direction.

"Collette Dunk, I haven't seen you in a long time!" he exclaimed. His slow smile rolled out to warm her. "Maybe I should ask Coli Duncan if she'd be willing to interview my band in *About Town*?"

"Actually, I came by for more personal reasons, but, ah, jazz is always of interest to my viewers. Mama Alphonse told me about her great-nephew, Orlando, jazz star of New Orleans. I just had to see if he was that skinny little senior from high school that I didn't have the nerve to talk to at the time."

"Guilty as charged, but I have to admit to not noticing any girls back then. I was so shy I just stuck my sax between me and reality," he replied with another smile.

They settled down to a hesitant talk about the folks that they remembered from the parish. Coli was reminded that Orlando's mama ran her own catering business. Sometimes he helped her by moving boxes of food and dishes from here to there. Probably accounting for some of his muscles. By the time they had moved on to what their friends and relatives were doing right now, Coli began to realize that maybe she did need to spend more time catching up. She liked the way Orlando listened to the comments she made. Before Coli really wanted the conversation to stop, Orlando was playing another set and she was in a taxi, heading home.

CHAPTER 4

FAMILIES MAKE OUR LIVES

Jubal Weekes, star of the Playmakers, was uneasy. He squared his shoulders and knocked on the front door of his childhood home. It needed a fresh coat of paint but he doubted that his parents had noticed. His sister, Tanora, opened it, gave him a hug and preceded him to the kitchen. His mama, Tuusa, turned from the sink and gave him a massive hug. It felt just as good as when he was six.

"Jubal, I'm so glad that you could come by." Tuusa's smile lit up her ample face. She was wrapped in a yellow apron that Jubal remembered from his childhood. Did she never buy anything for herself? He looked at the tawdry remnants of the kitchen curtains.

"Mama, I've missed you too." He sat down at the same wooden kitchen table. She went back to dishing up supper on the side board. "Do I need to give you a bit more so that you can finish the curtains and get them up?"

She turned and made a moue of embarrassment. "Giving me more might not move the curtain purchase along. You know Mrs. Chatterly with the six children and her husband Henry, who is not always the man he should be?"

"Yes, mama," Jubal replied with resignation. He had been here before.

"Well, she just needed a few things for the new baby so how could I not?"

"Suppose I gave you some more for the curtains?"

"Well, dear, you know how it is. So many parishioners and they often seem to need some help. I did pray to the Lord the last time and I really felt that he was directing me to Mrs. Chatterly."

"May the Lord's will be done," Jubal finished, trying hard not to be flippant.

"Call everyone to supper," his mother requested.

With much shuffling of chairs everyone squeezed in. It had been easier when they were smaller and fewer. His father, the Reverend Timothy Weekes, presided at the head of the table. His mother, Tuusa, at the foot. He and his sister, Tanora, were seated on the side with a good view of the twenty year old fridge and cluttered sideboard. Jordan and his new wife, Lucille, on the other side of the table were treated to the view outside, blue sky and wilted leaves. His father was in his black church suit but everyone else was wearing bright, cool clothes: an ample red flowered dress for mama and t-shirts and cut-offs for everyone else.

Rev. Weekes glared at Jubal but only said, "Let us bow our heads for the blessing. O Lord, forgive those of us who cannot appreciate your bounty by being on time for the wonderful food prepared for us here. We thank You for our health and the worship we bring to You. In God's name Amen."

Amens were echoed around the table and then everyone got down to the serious business of eating. His mother started passing the plates of wilted greens, succotash, ham and yams.

"Jordan," Tuusa looked his way. "How did that Conference go that you were preparing for?

"Pretty well." Jordan cautiously stretched his long legs under the table. "People seemed to be listening. I'm not sure that they're as worried about global warming, storms and sea level rise as I am. Too many of them want to believe Dr. Merriman who thinks these extreme hurricanes are just part of a natural up and down pattern."

"Don't you have the data to prove him wrong?" Reverent Weeks bent towards his son.

" Logical thinkers believe so, but they're mostly scientists. Lots of people are emotional thinkers who believe what they need to. Whatever makes them feel safe right now is what they believe." Jordan took a breath and sighed. " Worse storms and rising sea levels are not a future anyone wants."

"Coli Duncan did a pretty good report on the main ideas," ventured Lucille.

"Coli who?" asked the Reverend.

"You know, dear, Colette Dunc. She and her mother Charlene occasionally attend church," prompted Tuusa.

"Colette Dunc?" He turned the name around in his mind. "Oh yes, new reporter for Easy Times News. One of the many storm Christians."

"Now, dear."

"Sorry." His sons looked at him with interest. He was sheepish. "After every bad storm I have observed a strengthening of my congregation for awhile."

"She did do a good job," insisted Jordan. "So much so that I gave her my card and asked her to consider a program on the Restore Coastal Louisiana Now movement. I said that Lucille would be willing to give her a tour."

"Oh yes, now I remember her. She's using a different name now. At the end she talked to us. Pleasant, very enthusiastic. A cute little thing." He looked up to silence.

"Just because all of us look like our Maasai warrior ancestors is no reason to belittle her," Tanora couldn't stop herself from saying.

The silence rose up among them and swirled uneasily back and forth. Soft sounds of chewing and swallowing followed.

"I meant no disrespect," came quietly from Rev. Weekes. "Maybe she would come by and do a program on our fund raiser for repairing the levees?" he added to recover his audience.

"So, are you considering Jubal's offer of a new house in a better area?" asked Jordan, searching for another, more upbeat topic.

"No, no. My people are here. They need me to forgive their sins and help them seek God in their lives for strength. The poor need strength more than anyone."

"Ah, but the wealthy may have more sins to forgive, Dad." Jubal couldn't resist.

"That may be true, son, but if your wealth is a burden to you, you ask God's help. He might even suggest that you donate a sum to our church."

The sounds of more eating and passing of plates followed that oft heard suggestion.

"No Dad, I think I'll increase the fishes and loaves instead."

"Fishes and loaves?"

A Message from Katrina

"I'm not getting any younger. It's getting harder to break away down the court and hit the basket. Anytime in the next few years I could be injured or need to retire."

"But surely, you have money set by, son?" His mother was concerned.

"Yes, and I just spent a good portion of it buying a farm. Out near Uncle Thomas' place," Jubal finished, glaring at his father.

Coli watched Marc expertly ease his boat up to the dock. Lucille jumped onto the newly painted boards. Marc threw a dock line over to her. She quickly
cleated it. She made it seem easy. No doubt it was second nature for her. Then cousin Marc walked to the stern of the boat and tossed the second rope to her. They worked together like a well-oiled machine. You could tell they were cousins. Both were medium height, muscled and young, with sun-kissed skin. Lucille's black hair fitted right into the picture but Marc's straight brown hair must have come from a French ancestor.

Coli felt her city upbringing betraying her. Her mother would have been more at ease with boats and the bayou. She steeled herself to clamber over the edge onto the dock without too much loss to her dignity. She thought she would be better on the dock but it seemed to come up to meet her every time she took a step.

"See, there's what's left of the old dock," said Lucille pointing down at some submerged pilings. Coli could see them wavering under the surface of the water. They stretched quite a ways past the end of the present dock. It explained why Marc had made a point of coming in from the side instead of straight on.

Coli felt saddened at the loss of so much land and turned to look at the remaining island. The small house built on the highest point on the island was bravely painted blue with strong shutters and window frames outlined in white. Coli noted the ring of dying trees at the high tide line. Sad, soon they too would wash away with the storms and even more land would go with them. She focused on the door of the house where a small figure in a brightly flowered dress waved to them.

"There's Marie. Allons-y," continued Lucille.

"Bienvenue," called out Marie in a quavering voice. She peered closely at Coli. "Vous vous ressemblez à votre mère. Ah, oui, she was pretty like you and wanted to make something of herself, just like I hear you do."

While Coli was trying to connect that comment to the mother she knew, Lucille came forward, hugged Marie, and gave her the double kiss of greeting. Lucille allowed herself, Coli and Marc to be ushered into the kitchen where a table full of food awaited them. For quite some time the only sounds were those of friendly comments and appreciation for good food. When everyone was replete, they settled down to Coli's reason for coming.

"I've spent the last few days with Lucille," said Coli. "She's been showing me some of the work done by the *Restore Coastal Louisiana Now* group. We visited the Caernarvon Freshwater Diversion. It sure seems to have helped the freshwater fishermen hold onto the habitat of their catch species. Then we looked around at the mouth of the Go Canal. A lot of open water there. We saw all the traffic and the clear waterways and gas canals. Not much of a place for shrimp anymore."

"Not much of anything there except industry," muttered Lucille.

Coli turned to Marie, "Lucille told me that your husband was a shrimper. You probably knew my grandmother and grandfather."

"Ah, oui, I remember the old times. Not even that long ago. Was less than twenty-five, ben, less than twenty years, your grand-papa, Etienne, he was fishing. He was fishing with my man, Jerome. Lots of trips they took, good weather and not so good. They always got back, always, 'til the last time. Jerome, he called in. They had a good haul of shrimp, very good, maybe pay some of them bills. Home before dark, if a squall didn't catch them."

Marie looked up with pain in her eyes, even after all the years. "I never heard from them again. Next morning my brother, Charlie, and Marc's grandpapa, Luc went looking for them but they never found anything."

Marc interrupted her as if his patience had been all used up listening to the stories from his childhood one more time. "Yeah, must have been a water-spout got the boat. I know, and then things went from not good to even worse for all of us. Two more fishermen and one more boat just gone. Everybody left needing to work just a bit harder. It's the story of my time."

He stopped suddenly, as if he had said too much. His face turned red with trying to keep his anger packed away because letting it go wouldn't change anything. He'd still be too young and too poor in a dying fishery and a fading lifestyle. He glared at Coli. "All the reporters this side of Hell won't fix any of it."

Coli knew she had to diffuse his anger or they would have a very uncomfortable trip back to Leesville. "You've been studying the fishing industry as well as working with your father." At his reluctant nod Coli continued, "Lucille took me out to see the Caernarvon Freshwater Diversion Project on the Atchafalaya River. It seemed to be pretty effective in slowing down the flow. Seems like it allows the silt in the river to build and repair sandbars and islands."

"Yeah, if we had a few more of the diversions and less of the canals and gas line channels cut out of bayous, Marie might not have needed a new dock. Yeah, and some of the acres of spartina grass I planted might still be growing." Marc's face was starting to turn red and he was trying hard not to shout. Lucille started to look worried. Then, she pasted a smile on her face for Marie.

"Coli needs to leave now, Marie. Thanks for the visit. Come on, Marc, you need to get back too." She hustled all of them out with barely a backward glance.

As they were walking down to the boat Coli asked, "What just happened there?"

Silence flowed around them. Finally, Marc answered, "Lucille's just protecting me. She knows when I'm ready to blow. Another minute and Marie would have been telling you about how the whole family made sure I went to school so I could save the fishing and everybody's way of life. Yeah, me, the big hope. I believed it too until I knew too much. Building islands, one spartina root at a time. I wish I had a better idea." He stepped into the boat and started the engine. Coli followed him, not daring to say anything. Lucille uncleated the lines and threw them aboard.

Coli looked out to the water, blue waves dancing beneath blue skies. She had thought how beautiful it was coming out.   Now she could only see how much was missing.

Coli opened one eye with a huge effort.   Yes, that was sunshine out there.   Ten o'clock already.   Hurray for Saturday mornings after late Friday nights, after a week of too much work and too little everything else.   Okay, take stock.   Her eyes wandered around her tiny apartment.   It was amazing how much could be piled on each flat surface when she wasn't even here most of the time.   Groceries— buy some.   Phone—wink, wink—a message she could no longer avoid.   She approached it with some trepidation as she had forgotten to phone her mother for a week, no, maybe a month.   No, even that last nasty message hadn't motivated her to do it.

She felt her familiar anger and guilt surfacing.   She had left a message about her trip to the Bayou, about how she wanted to find out more about her grandfather's death. Maybe things her mother should have told her long since. She had always needed to know more about her mama's family, but all her questions had been met with silence or very short answers.   She mentally defended herself.   She was just too busy with her job, especially her trip to the bayou, and her friends.   Well, maybe just her job lately.

A Message from Katrina

Coli used to spend more time with friends. She remembered friends from high school, friends from college but somehow she just hadn't had time to spend with them lately. Well, that could be fixed. Look at how she'd enjoyed Orlando's music and conversation. She wasn't a hopeless workaholic. But that light was still winking at her and she really did want to talk to her mother about her visit with Marie. She reached over with uneasiness roiling in her stomach.

"Where the hell are you and why haven't you phoned? You can't work all the time. Even a trip to the Bayou can't take that long. Your hair looked awful in your last ghost background. Edna and I have carved out some time for you on Saturday at 4:00. Get here and we won't even charge you." Then her voice changed and she said softly, "I miss you, Collette."

Mothers, they sure know how to push the guilt button. Maybe she could fit it all in today if she leaped out of bed right now. She caught a glimpse of her hair in the mirror. Maybe her mother was right for once.

Coli wiped the sweat from her forehead. It sure was hot this August, even for someone born and raised in hot, someone who always wondered what tourists were whining about. Mama's hair salon looked just a little bit more rundown and a little bit sadder every time she came by. Well, no surprise, Edna was getting on and her mother wasn't exactly Mrs. Home Depot. Neither was Coli, for that matter.

She pushed the door open and entered into the smell of her childhood, a bouquet of mingled perfumes. Within it were the chemical smells of ammonia, shampoo and setting gels. Her mother was wiping the counter at her station. She was a small Cajun woman who looked younger every time Coli saw her. Masses of curly dark hair, just like Orlando's, thought Coli with a smile; not that her mama would like the comparison.

Charlene gathered up her combs and dropped them into the glass of disinfectant. Coli had spent far more time here than she had ever wanted to. Cute little Collette playing in the back while her mother worked. Be nice to the customers, quiet and polite was the constant mantra. She headed over to the sink to do her penance.

Turning at the sound of the door, Charlene saw Coli coming in and asked: "How was your trip to the Bayou? Happy now that you found your roots?"

"It's good to see you too, Mama" replied Coli, surprised once more at how her mother could irritate her just by opening her mouth. Coli tried to keep the accusation out of her voice as she said, "Why didn't you ever tell me more stories about your family and your childhood? Why didn't you tell me that you left because your father died?"

"Because I didn't."

"That's what Marie Laveau told me."

"Saloppe, coo-yon," muttered Charlene.

Coli sighed. "She was old, but she wasn't dirty or foolish. You've avoided talking to me about this for long enough. I'm an adult now. You can tell me the truth."

Charlene looked surprised. "I never told you because there weren't nothing to tell." Charlene stopped. She looked into the distance of memory and sighed. "It were a long time ago. My papa went out shrimping and never came back. It weren't nothing out of the ordinary. Lots of boats go down. One minute he was saying that he'd be home for supper on the marine band, especially if the winds of the approaching storm gave him a little push. He never came home."

Charlene looked at Coli from eyes that really weren't focused on the present. "Mama and me waited up most of the night. We never talked about what we feared."

Charlene sighed again. "Next morning Marie's brother, Charles, and his friend, Luc, looked where they figured the boat would have been. Nothing. They found nothing."

She stopped again but Coli didn't say anything, silenced by the pain in her mother's voice. Maybe pain had been keeping her mother silent all these years.

After a pause of regret Charlene started again: "Everybody said it must have been a waterspout got the boat. It was heavy with shrimp. What a good catch he had on ice in the hold. We needed the money." She stopped again, still in the past. Then she roused herself and looked Coli in the face. "But that weren't why I left."

"What was it then?" asked Coli, genuinely puzzled.

"It weren't even that my mother was dying of cancer. I didn't know that then. Mama just said she was feeling poorly again and wanted to stay with her sister in Leeville for awhile."

"Did you feel abandoned?" Coli felt her new sympathy for her mother continuing to grow.

"No, no," Charlene insisted. "You got it all wrong. I was glad to leave. You know the feeling of wanting to leave someone you ought to love." Charlene glared at Coli. "I was glad to leave. Mama was trying to help me. I was desperate to get away. Every day the same as the last. All those potluck dinners at the church hall, surrounded by aunts, uncles, and cousins. All those mountains of good cooking. Every woman so proud of her cooking. Mutters behind my back. Pauvre T-Charlee, her mama's sick again. Ben, she tries her best and her red beans are getting better."

"But why?   Everybody was friendly to me, especially when they found out I was T- Charlee's daughter. And the food was great."

"It's all about family."   Charlene sighed again. "Mama and Papa wanted a big family. I was the first and then there was going to be lots of boys to go shrimping and lots of girls to help Mama. As a kid I didn't understand at first. Mama and Papa would be pleased then Mama would be sick and then it would happen again and again.   I couldn't make it better. I wasn't enough."

"Enough what?" asked Coli.

Charlene didn't answer for a while. Finally she said, "I know now that Mama had miscarriage after miscarriage." Her voice faded out. Her eyes took on a far away look.

Coli felt herself getting angry again. "So you came to the Big Easy to find excitement?"

"Yeah, I did," said Charlene with a finality that signalled that her uncharacteristic touchy-feely time was over. Charlene reverted to her usual caustic self. "You can sneer but I was only fifteen and I thought anywhere would be better.   I was lucky to get a job with Edna. Her daughters taught me a thing or two." She steered Coli over to a sink.

"But not enough to see through Ed. How I loved that man, all the clubs he took me to and the dancing. Oh, the excitement of it all. I fell for him like Papa's ship going down and never came up for air. Nope, glub, glub 'til he was gone and you were crying at my knee."

"So, now it's all my fault?" protested Coli as Charlene attached the plastic cape at the back of her neck and started the water running.

"No, it isn't always about you. No, I grieved for Ed, and my own stupid dreams of a perfect future. I tried not to blame you but you were always there. Always needing me to do something, feed you, change your diapers, sing you to sleep. It was just too much. I'm sorry. I knew I wasn't fair to you but I just couldn't..." her voice trailed off. Her hands stilled and she stared off in space as the water continued to run.

Coli watched her and realized, for the first time in her life, that her mother had been sixteen, pregnant and on her own. Suddenly she saw herself at fifteen and sixteen with friends in school. Her biggest problem, aside from her mother, was getting to her waitressing job on time.

Charlene suddenly came back to herself and started vigorously shampooing Coli's hair as she carped, "You won't come to see me but a free hair-cut, that's something different. Searching around for a less personal subject, she continued, "You don't really believe all that weather stuff about global warming and the end of the Bayou, do you?"

A Message from Katrina

Coli heard Edna come out from the backroom. She loved the smile in Edna's voice as she said: "Hi, Collette. What your mama, bless her heart, really wants to say is 'I'm proud of your work'. She just can't quite get it out."

"Don't you be putting words in my mouth, Edna. This girl never did appreciate all I done for her."

Edna walked past them wheezing, smoking yet one more cigarette. She winked behind Coli's mother's back and lowered herself into her chair with relief. Her ankles looked even more puffy than usual. Coli made a point of not looking at them.

"You've been doing pretty good on the cable lately, Collette. I've even started to watch it for more than just the channel choices," said Edna. Her simple words thrilled Coli. Maybe all her hard work and all the hours were worth it. She'd show them that she wasn't just the sometimes-neglected daughter of a drunk. Then she looked at her mother in the mirror snipping with concentration and felt guilty.

The guilt didn't overcome her simmering feelings of anger. She really had to talk to her mother again about what she had found out about her grandparents. Nothing she had found out either today or from Marie was so awful that it accounted for her mother's determined silence over the years.

Coli leaned her head back with a sigh. She felt good. She was wearing her version of the classic black shirt and pants with swinging silver earrings and necklace. Her hair really did look better after her mother's efforts. She was tucked behind a small table and was moving her feet to the music. She didn't know whether Orlando had noticed that she was here yet, and, at the moment, didn't really care.

She should get out more. The two different guys she had discouraged from joining her had boosted her confidence and the one drink she had allowed herself was making her pleasantly mellow. This set was winding down and the lights were slowly coming up. Orlando stopped playing, stretched, spoke briefly to the other guys in the band and did a slow look around the club. He spotted her and made a slow advance through friends and conversations toward her. He didn't rush, but he didn't change direction either. Somehow that built up her anticipation.

Orlando spread his slow smile over her and said, " You're looking good tonight, Coli. Your mother attack your hair again?"

She replied, "I can only say 'No' to her for so long."

Basking in Orlando's smile, Coli thought that this was the guy she did want to encourage.

A Message from Katrina

"So, how y'all doin' Coli?" asked Orlando, settling in close to her on the padded bench seat.

She looked up at him, enjoying his soft smile, dark sparkling eyes, and close cut curly hair. The suggestion of muscles under his loose shirt was something she would explore later, she promised herself. Orlando was still waiting for her reply so she tried to pull herself together. "I've been busy at work," she managed to reply. His raised eyebrows and interested expression gave her permission to go on.

"Did you see my report on the weather conference?" she asked. At his nod she continued, "Well, Jordan Weekes gave me his card and his wife, Lucille, who is a member of the *Restore Coastal Louisiana Now*, called me. I just spent four days with her doing interviews."

Orlando watched her animated features and listened to her describing the Barrier Islands, or what was left of them. He did like a woman who had something interesting to talk about. Too many hours had been spent hearing his sisters chatter on about make-up and clothes. Orlando tuned back in and realized that he'd just been asked a question. "Sorry," he managed.

"Orlando," repeated Coli. "Did you ever hear anything about organizing tours of the Barrier Islands?" As Orlando seemed to be searching his memory, Coli wrapped her fingers around the chair seat and tried to stop talking.

"About a year after I started at the agency, the old boss retired and turned the business over to his daughter. There was a retirement party and he talked about his challenges and achievements, as he put it. Well, one of his challenges had been the loss of the Barrier Island tours. He said when he first started the agency they had organized boat tours out as far as Dernières Isles to see some of the deserted homes and hotels. They stopped them because the water was creeping higher and higher and the tourists found the whole scene depressing, rather than historical and romantic. Then, he realized that he could substitute alligator farm tours. He bragged about how popular they had been over the last twenty years."

"I guess people who come all this way don't come to be depressed but to have a good time," mused Coli. "I guess they don't want to think about global warming, carbon dioxide levels rising and airplane exhausts."

Orlando tickled Coli in the ribs. "Cut out that kind of talk. I like my day job. I couldn't afford to be playing here if tourists weren't coming to the Big Easy." He looked toward the stage and saw his band members starting to set up. "I've got another set, Coli, if you can stay." Coli couldn't stifle a huge yawn.

"It's not your company or the music," Coli said. "But I really did have a busy week and I must leave now or I'll fall asleep on the bus."

A Message from Katrina

Orlando started to panic. He had watched for her to turn up at the club for too many nights already. He had to come up with a date idea and a cheap one at that. Orlando looked towards the stage and saw the other band members getting ready to start. He gave Coli his most persuasive smile and tried his sudden inspiration.

"You were talking about Rev. Weekes and his mission about fixing the levees. How about meeting me at the Baptist church tomorrow and we can see if he's still on about that?" It seemed lame but it was the only plan he had right now.

Coli didn't really want to go to church but she really did want to see Orlando again. She smiled her 'yes' at him and looked up to tell him more but he was already heading for the stage. She felt disappointed as she gathered up her stuff to leave.

When Orlando looked up from the band's first number he didn't see Coli in their corner. He put his frustrations and longing into the music. The enthusiastic applause at the end of the number was a surprise. As Orlando played on his thoughts returned to how to increase Coli's interest in him. He was glad she had said 'yes' to church but he was already thinking of an interview about his band. Maybe that would give him another reason to see her.

CHAPTER 5

RELIGIOUS VISIONARY OR CRAZY?

Coli felt as if she could have slept all day but she wanted to meet Orlando before the service. She felt a little tingle of excitement that she hadn't felt for far too long. Even a very boring church service would be improved if she were seated beside Orlando.

She struggled off the bus. She looked up to the levee and could see a ship passing majestically between the treetops and the skyline. All that weight of water made her shudder and think, "Please, not today." Visions of water racing over the levee and swirling her away returned to her from her childhood fears. She pushed them away with adult logic. It was a perfectly fine summer day. She let her eyes roam over the trees framing the church and flowerbeds in full blossom. Orlando was slumped against the church gate, looking like this morning had arrived too soon.

A Message from Katrina

The music was strong and the voices blended and soared with enthusiasm. Everyone sat down with a rustling and bumping of bodies. Reverend Weekes stood behind his pulpit. He started off in a booming voice: "Today I will read from Exodus Chapter 9, Verse *1:* Then the LORD said unto Moses, Go in unto Pharaoh, and tell him, Thus saith the LORD God of the Hebrews, Let my people go, that they may serve me.*

"You might wonder what the exodus from Egypt has to do with your life in these times. Everyday we wake up in the morning and we look at the Levee and it is still there. Sometimes we see the ships sailing over our heads because it is still there. We say a prayer for the miracles that man has created because it is still there. But, the miracles of men have a price. As you know, I have been petitioning, pushing, and prodding every elected official that I could for the last fifteen years to have those levees repaired and upgraded. Eleven years ago we had a bill before Congress but this president, THIS PRESIDENT, I say, found other more pressing projects for our tax dollars.

"We have been crying in the wilderness and waiting for a sign, lo these many years. I have wrestled with this demon again and again. Well, I am a modern man. I am your pastor, but I am also a proud and stubborn man. So, when I had my dream the first time, I ignored it as too much rich food. But, the Lord did not give up. No, the Lord does not give up on us sinners.

"The second dream I put down to exhaustion, stress, and fear, but the Lord did not give up. He sent my son, Jubal, to me with a farmer's vision, of all things. The third dream was exactly the same as the first two. A tortured voice cries out above the noise of the storm, "Let my people go from the chains that bind them, their greed, and ease, and fear. Let my people go and lead them to the Promised Land." Then, the noise of the wind rises, and the screams of people in panic rise. Then, a huge wave of water rushes over us.

"I awoke from the terror of my dream and I prayed to the Lord. He has given me a daunting task to save my people, but I am ready with His help to do it. We will be the first urban group to resettle the agricultural small towns of America. Come after the Service to a meeting in the hall to hear more.

"Let us pray—O Lord, give us the strength and the vision for this immense undertaking. Amen"

The choir and the congregation took up the last hymn with a dazed fervor and then everyone streamed over to the hall.

A Message from Katrina

Coli took a big bite out of her muffaletta, catching the drip with her tongue. Orlando savored the bitter and strong café-au-lait. They had rejected the meet and greet in the church hall in favour of a table for two here outside the café. The indifferent crowd was passing on the street just inches from their table. "Man, is that Reverend Weekes of yours crazy!"

"Some of the folks at the service were taking him seriously. It looks like his son has already bought a farm and now he's talking about building condos in the town of Grand Falls," said Orlando.

"So, he's surrounding himself with crazies as well," Coli laughed.

"He may be, but I've got you, at least for awhile," smiled back Orlando. Then he asked, "You got a vision, Coli? You know, like something you really want to do?"

Coli looked hesitantly at Orlando and then watched the crowd pass for a minute or two. She said in a low voice, "Yeah, actually I do." There was silence while she decided how much to say. "I want to be the media journalist that everybody knows and trusts. You know, the person who explains every disaster so that you feel that you understand what's going on. The knowing makes you feel better, like you can cope with it, no matter how bad it is. Mind you, having it happening miles away from your comfortable chair helps too."

"You mean someone like Walter Cronkite was for my mama and like Roger Silverfox is for me?"

"Especially Roger Silverfox. He's been my role model for a long time. He's so knowledgeable and caring. I feel safe listening to him."

Orlando looked up at Coli and smiled shyly. She mentally kicked herself for being so self-centred. "So, what's your vision, Orlando?"

"I hope it's more than a vision by now. I've been working and saving for a long time. No money for a big date for a long time, maybe too long." He smiled at Coli.

"You're going to start a jazz school in Polynesia?"

"Might as well be." He smiled back. "Actually, I saved almost enough now that I can start looking for somewhere cheap to start my own club."

"Your own club?"

"Yeah, but not today. Suppose we take a little stroll around Audubon Park and enjoy some of this sunshine before we're both back at work?" Orlando stood up and drew Coli up with him. She couldn't say "yes" fast enough.

Jubal took up both seats near the back of the bus. The trip to their first exhibition game after training camp seemed extra long this year. He was excited about buying the Cuthbert's farm and a little worried about his plans for the condo complex. Maybe he had bit off more than he could chew.

He had talked to his uncle about the idea. After Thomas had gotten over his surprise he had said that he had always known that Jubal's basketball career was only the beginning. At least his uncle was proud of him, even if everybody else thought he was crazy.

He had told his Dad, but only received a surprised look in return. Generally, his Dad worried about his immortal soul, with all the money he was making. Hah, most other parents would be falling on his neck in gratitude. Not his Dad though. He still couldn't accept that neither one of his sons had heard the Call of the Lord. Mention of money always elicited the story of Christ and the moneylenders in the temple. Fortunately his mama quietly pocketed the odd gift with a smile and a hug. It probably went directly to one more needy family, knowing her.

The image of his mother got him to thinking about marrying. The older he got the more he wondered how life on the road and a wife would combine. It wasn't the lack of women that was a problem. No, they threw themselves in his path so frequently that he barely noticed their differences. Under his sport jock exterior he was really a romantic. He needed to find a woman that he had to pursue, and find a way to make her notice him. He gave himself a mental kick in the ass. Get real, he concluded.

The noise of this year's crop of new players razzing Kincaid echoed down the bus. Jubal heard the bite of Kincaid's reply and realized that the new guys didn't know when to stop. He and Kincaid had battled many times at one of the park's battered baskets before giving up in exhaustion. The only difference was that he had kept growing after he turned twelve and Kincaid hadn't. He'd better intervene before blood was splattered. "Hey, Kincaid, got a problem back here," he called out. Kincaid pulled back his raised fist and walked back to Jubal amid catcalls and laughter. "You'll soon have them whipped into shape," Jubal said as Kincaid slammed his body into the seat beside him.

"It gets harder every year to make those self-centred super stars into a team. They don't appreciate what I do. Neither do you. It's not just about the equipment."

"Actually, I do know what you do. I know we're winning more games because everything is where it should be when it should be. No headaches about equipment or schedules ever."

"Yeah, but not as glamorous as sinking that last basket. I think I've been doing this for too long. Do you ever feel like you need a change, Jubal?" Kincaid's banter had left him and he stared earnestly at Jubal.

A Message from Katrina

"You know that farm I bought as my retirement project?" At Kincaid's nod he continued, "My farm consultant has been whining at me that he needs more help. I can't do it. I'm away playing ball too often, earning all that money that just seems to be running through my fingers since I bought a farm." Kincaid nodded again, not really understanding where the conversation was going. "I really need someone there I can trust. Someone who's good at keeping track of things, doing accounts and telling me what's really going on." Kincaid suddenly caught on.

"I'll think about it," he said.

"Now, get back there and start whipping this year's team into shape. I can't do it all by myself," Jubal ended, giving Kincaid a friendly shove on his shoulder.

Jubal watched Kincaid lurch back to the front of the bus. The two of them had been a team for a long time. He had helped Kincaid get his first job as equipment manager for the Playmakers. He'd watched his friend's mind clicking and whirring through all those extension accountancy courses. He shuddered at the thought. That kind of thing made no sense to him.

Oh no, Miles was ambling towards the seat beside him. When Jubal was feeling paranoid (and who wasn't sometimes) he saw this kid as his biggest competition on the team. Miles was hungry, and he had incredible skills. All he lacked was experience and the ability to act the star.

He still expressed puppyish admiration, maybe sincere, or maybe a good camouflage.

"Jubal, mind if I sit with you?" he asked.

"No, glad to see yuh," grunted Jubal, "You made the difference in the last quarter yesterday at practice."

"Only because of your passes," replied Miles enthusiastically.

"We're the team," replied Jubal with the obligatory high five. Now that the little ritual was done they could get down to business.

Miles looked both ways. "I'm wanting to buy a house for mama," he said, looking to Jubal for support.

"Better than parties or women," replied Jubal.

"Yeah, but how and where?" questioned Miles.

"My advice probably isn't worth much," muttered Jubal. "When I tried to buy a new place for my mama and papa, my Dad flatly refused to consider moving away from his parish. I told him that the poor weren't the only ones needing to be saved. I said that maybe the wealthy were even bigger sinners but he wouldn't budge. He told me that he didn't need my money or my stupid ideas." Jubal shrugged his shoulders in defeat.

"Least you got a Dad to fight with," snorted Miles. "My Dad was long gone by the time I realized that some dads stuck around."

A Message from Katrina

"Anyways, the house … your mama … " prompted Jubal realizing that both of them were sliding into bitter thoughts. Then, he suddenly thought of Grand Falls and the places that a couple of other team members had already bought there. "Does your mama like your basketball career?" he questioned. This might work out after all. He leaned towards Miles with new enthusiasm, thinking of all the hopes he had for his farm and the future of Grand Falls.

CHAPTER 6

EXODUS ON A SUNDAY

Coli still couldn't believe it. She had been so busy for the last two weeks that she had barely had time to look up. Work had consumed her. She was proud of the programs she had put together. Coli Duncan would be a household name very soon she vowed. However, she hadn't had a chance to go by and see Orlando. He hadn't called which disappointed her more than she had any right to feel. She also hadn't phoned her mother yet. So, when her Mama had actually called last night, she had found her palms sweating and her heart pounding away with guilt. Charlene had sounded sober and sane on the phone so when she suggested a Sunday bus trip to Grand Falls with the other interested parishioners, guilt had made Coli accept.

Beside her mother on the bus, Coli watched all that water and the mostly flat landscape pass by. This wasn't a first. There had been times in the past when Charlene had rode on the wagon. Sometimes for a week or two, sometimes for a month or two. Coli always thought of them as the cruelest of times because she would just start hoping or imagining what life could be like with a normal mother and she would come home to find her mama slumped on the sofa drunk and unconscious. Drunk and raving were worse though because it was always Coli's fault that Charlene had started to drink again.

Stop it. Stop it, she told herself. Just enjoy today. You can't fix tomorrow anymore than yesterday. She turned her gaze outside the window again. Still farm fields —some kind of row crops. God, the countryside was dreary. What did people do out here? Commune with their soybeans? Probably not if they were GMO crops. She remembered the documentary she had put together. The links alleged between the government agencies and big seed companies had been truly frightening.

Her mother shifted and fluttered her eyelids. "Are we there yet?" she demanded.

"Not yet, but soon. We've been on the road for almost two hours so we should be almost there," Coli replied.

The bus went over the top of a slight rise and a valley with a river winding through it was laid out before them. The bus slowed down and pulled off the road near an entrance to THE RIVERSIDE CAMPGROUNDS AND RV PARK. A skinny young dark-skinned guy with a big Afro and glasses walked toward the bus. He climbed aboard, straightened up to his full and unprepossessing height and said, "Hi folks, I'm Kincaid Duval, Jubal's farm accountant. I've got the job of giving you a guided tour of Grand Falls and then you'll have a couple of hours to look around on your own before the buses head back to town."

"We'll start with a stroll up to the falls. I bet that y'all wouldn't mind a bit of a stretch about now." With that Coli, Charlene and the others started to stand up and move off the bus.

They walked through willows providing welcome shade from the heat of the mid-day sun. The trail was pleasant and slowly drew them uphill to the Falls. Two small streams pooled out from behind a large boulder and trickled over the edge of a minimal drop down to a small river. "This is Grand Falls?" exclaimed Coli in consternation.

"Perhaps the first settlers had a rich sense of the ridiculous. Maybe they were just realists." Kincaid deliberately let his gaze swing in a full circle around their group. From this slight rise, all that could be seen were fields, farms, and a few roads. No other falls graced their vision.

The rest of the tour was equally disappointing. The main street of town did have some old, spreading trees lining it but their leaves were dusty and limp. The trees themselves rose above older houses and storefronts, most in need of paint and hope. There did seem to be some new businesses in town. One of them seemed to have recycled the old tobacco warehouse for producing paving "stones" from chewed up and recycled running shoes. The scenes seemed to be going from curious to curiouser.

Coli craned her head around as she came down the steps of the bus. Yes, she had caught a glimpse of Orlando. He was surrounded by his family, his mother, his four sisters and several of his nieces and nephews. He turned and saw her. His expression became one of longing and excitement. He called out, "Coli, am I ever glad that you're here. "   His family turned as one and looked at her in surprise.

Her mother pulled her aside and hissed, "Are you seeing Orlando, Collette?"

"Well, I haven't seen all of him yet", Coli answered with an attempt at humour.

"This is not a joke," hissed Charlene. "Don't let his skin fool you. He's a nigger, you know."

You certainly couldn't accuse her mother of being colourblind. Coli tried one more attempt at humour. "Do you think he's too good for white trash like us, Mama?" she asked with a smile.

Her mother looked mortally offended. She turned around with indignation in every line of her body and marched off down the street, heading for *The Honkey-Tonk*

Bar. Coli followed reluctantly. It was going to be her fault again when her mother fell off the wagon.

She opened the door and entered the dimly lit back of the barroom. It had a cowboy theme. The décor was western, old and dusty but that hadn't stopped her mother. She was already sipping her drink. Coli gave up and ordered a beer. She wasn't a child any more and had no extra energy to rail against the inevitable. The day had gotten too hot and she was thirsty.

Charlene had managed to down two beers by the time Coli finished her first. Charlene started to motion for another when Coli capitulated and said with a sigh.

"Orlando and I are not "intimate" Mama if that's what you want to hear." Although more from lack of time, than from lack of interest on her part she thought. When her mama still refused to acknowledge her statement Coli gave up. She grabbed her mother by the elbow and hurried out of the bar. "Come on Mama, we want to see something of this town." Charlene looked mutinous but came along with only a bit of quiet muttering.

The main street had seen better days. One third of the shops was functional but not thriving. One third was in a flourish of renovations. One third was empty. There was the failed mini-mall with a few stores still limping along. Even the big box store had closed down some time ago and insisted its customers follow it to Baton Rouge. As they passed the big steel structure they saw that it had been renamed Grand Falls Centre. One section was now called The Timothy Weekes Auditorium.

"Let's go in and see what they've done so far," said Coli. They came into the back of a large room with chairs set out facing a raised stage with a lectern on it. Reverend Weekes was behind it. Charlene said, "That man is the reason I go to church. I know I don't go that regular but he is a treat to listen to". Coli could feel his charisma reaching out to her as well. They slid into two chairs at the back to listen for a while.

Reverend Weekes' voice rang out. "Yes, the Lord works in mysterious ways. When my son was a teenager and a young man it grieved my soul that he was not willing to follow my calling and help spread the gospel. Many times I lost my temper and insisted that he stop playing ball and spend more time at his studies.

"It astounded me and shamed me that he refused again and again to follow the Christian and sensible future that I had laid out for him. For many years his selfish and hedonistic choices made a rift between us. "But, God works in His own ways and at His own purposes. When Jubal first came to me with his plans to buy a farm in Grand Falls I was astounded and pleased to see that he was making some adult choices. When his team members started buying up land and businesses around Grand Falls I began to understand his vision for a sustainable local economy and a repopulated town.

"When I came home from lobbying for funds to refurbish the levees, I was exhausted and dispirited from the lack of response at any level of government. I had been trying for years to convince anyone of our desperate need. I fell into an exhausted sleep that night and once again dreamed of winds and storms and rising waters.

" I saw Moses in my dream, lifting his staff and leading his people. I expected him to say, 'Let my people go', but instead he cried out, 'Bring my people forth to a new life in a new place.' When Jubal phoned the next morning to tell me that he was now the owner of a large farm, the scales fell from my eyes and I saw God's plan revealed clearly.

"Now, today, you have had a chance to see the possibilities that this town holds for us. Let us thank the Lord in prayer for this chance at a new beginning."

Coli and her mother eased themselves out the back door after the prayer ended. They sauntered back to the main street and continued their explorations. One of the older houses caught their attention. The front door and porch were newly painted a soft pink. Above the steps, a daintily painted sign heralded *Cost Effective Cuts*. A discreet paper sign by the door said, *HELP WANTED INQUIRE WITHIN.* "I think I'll go in," said Charlene.

A Message from Katrina

"Why?" asked Coli. "You and Edna have been partners and friends for years."

"For a reporter you sure don't notice much," sneered her mother. "Couldn't you see how bad Edna was last time we did your hair?

Coli thought her mother always tried to tear her down. She hissed back, "I'm focused, Mama. I'm focused on my job. It takes time and commitment to do it."

Charlene hardly noticed her interruption. She swept right on. "Edna's talking about retiring and we've discussed selling the business because I don't want to be left on my own. You've never been willing to support me and take up a career in hairdressing," she finished with malice.

Coli sighed. To her the words 'career' and 'hairdressing' shouldn't appear in the same sentence. She followed her mother into the shop to the old-fashioned tinkle of the bell at the front door. The shop room was small, tidy and decorated in shades of pink.

The walls were adorned with fading photos of hairstyles from the eighties. A slight, older woman, crowned in a halo of blue-rinsed grey curls came in from the back room. She smiled at them and said with the soft slow vowels of the south. "What can I do for y'all?"

Charlene tried her best for a smile as she looked around the room and winced at the décor. Maybe this shop

77

was just too genteel for her. "I'm interested in your help wanted sign", she tried in her most cultured voice.

" I'm Grace McTavish. I've worked here on my own for the last twenty years since my husband died. I've watched my business slowly fade as families have moved away for the big cities," she said sadly.

Then she brightened up and went on, "but lately we've had all these new young people come to town. They tell me that they want to have their hair cut locally. I confess that I have not kept up with all the new trends and I need someone more, (she hesitated delicately) 'with it', to help with the new business. Imagine," she went on, "men coming in here and expecting me to cut their hair," she finished in an amazed tone.

Coli could see her mother trying hard not to roll her eyes in amusement. The two women murmured on about the business. Coli tried her best to block out the excruciating details and amused herself by trying to date the hairstyles in the photographs.

Finally, she noticed that there was a general exodus to the back room. She followed slowly and stopped in surprise in the doorway. Maybe there was hope for her mother to find common ground with Mrs. Nice. The room was comfortably untidy. Cigarette butts were in danger of overtopping several shell-shaped ashtrays. A few beer bottles and cans were discreetly arranged in one corner of the kitchen counter. Coli caught bits of the conversation, "need to relax…small suite with an entrance from the back porch". She couldn't stand it any more. She felt she was going to fade away from terminal boredom. She rallied her best smile and said, "If you'll excuse me, I think I'll just explore around town a bit more. I'll meet you in about half an hour at the *Broken Cup* for supper, Mama. Nice meeting you, Grace." She eased out the door with as much friendliness as she could muster.

Coli yawned, as she looked out the bus windows in the gathering dusk. She had walked around town but had not seen either Orlando or his family. She had enjoyed the light meal in the local diner, which seemed to be in the throes of expanding to double its original size. Her mother had only admitted to considering joining the Cost Effective Cuts staff team at some indistinct future date. It was a pity she always found time spent with her mother so pointless and exhausting.

Next week at work promised to be busy. Coli had completed the work of editing the interviews and shots she had taken in her four days with Lucille. Their visit to the Barrier Islands had been worked up into a good program and she needed to talk to George at work tomorrow about scheduling it. Maybe she should try to catch a short nap on the way home.

Everyone was streaming out of the buses into the semi-dark of the parking lot near the church. Coli and her mother had gone their separate ways when she felt a soft pat on her back. "See you soon at the club, Coli?" whispered Orlando in her ear as he passed quickly on the fringe of his family group.

CHAPTER 7

THE BIG BREAK

How could it be Wednesday night already? Coli wiped the sweat off her brow as she struggled with the key in her door, the purse over her shoulder and the grocery bag cradled in one arm. The end of August could be just too hot! By this time of day everything stuck to everything else.

Yes, Coli had meant to go by the club and see Orlando and yes, she had spent more time thinking about him than their limited time together seemed to warrant, but it was already mid-week and she had done nothing but work. Programming took time, and research took more time and the boss had started to talk about retirement. So that probably meant getting used to a new boss soon. Whoa! *If* she kept her job was an unwelcome thought which had just popped into her head.

Since Coli had been thirteen she had thought that getting her own job and getting out of Mama's house would make life a dream. Now, she realized that the pressures never stopped. In dreams and awake, her mind was going in several directions at once. Her boss, George, had agreed that the Barrier Island program could be entitled *Saving Ourselves with Islands* and he would try to air it next week.

Could she rest and enjoy the results of her hard work? Could she think about all she had learned by talking to so many people? What about the sinking land, the diminishing fisheries, and the economic importance of the gas and oil industry? She wanted to take time to think about who was responsible and what could be done. But no, she had had to rush off to the church to interview Rev. Weekes at his media event.

That interview had grabbed everyone's attention. Even Edna had phoned her to comment on it. She could still see the front of the church, partially blocked by a large scaffold. It was made of three platforms. On the top one, about twenty feet in the air, the children in the choir were wearing their dark maroon choir gowns. The bottom two platforms contained the choir members in costumes—many wore bright orange lifejackets, but the rest were dressed as fish! They were lovely fish, resplendent in shimmering scales of brown, green and silver. Rev. Weekes made the point that if money wasn't earmarked for fixing the levees, this would be the situation in his parish. Only the top row at the twenty foot level would be above the water level. All the rest of the congregation would be either floating or fish. Then, she had captured the chorus and a verse of "The New Earth Song". She still remembered its folksong rhythm but chilling words.

It's taken far too many years,
And far too many tears,
To conquer all our fear,
And see the message clear.
Our future can be bright
 If we treat our planet right.
 And we can carry on, can carry on
Yes, we can!

Hurricanes roared in to break them,
Coastal cities, rich and proud.
Shattered bits among the high tides
Was all the future, storms allowed.

Click! Her key wouldn't turn in the lock. She tried to refocus her mind on the present and realized that she was using her office door key. Get a grip! As she inserted the correct key, she heard her phone ring.

Hurry, hurry, she thought. She finally unlocked her door to the sound of the phone still ringing. Slamming the door shut, she bounded across the room and dragged the receiver to her ear. She heard her mother's strident tones.

"About time! I've been trying to get you all day! Edna died yesterday. Her family is having the funeral on Friday. I expect you to be there." She went on about the details, but Coli barely heard them through her shock. Edna had looked ill when she had last seen her, but now that Coli really thought about it, Edna hadn't really looked well for a long time.

She had been such a feature in Coli's life for so long that she hadn't ever imagined a time when Edna wouldn't be there for her. Coli had always liked the way she had quietly been a support when her mother was raving. It might even have been Edna who first helped Coli understand that she didn't need to be an adult like her mama or even a hairdresser.

Coli finally managed to mutter, "I'm very sorry to hear about Edna's death." She gathered all her courage and said, "Is there anything I can do to help?"

"No, of course not," sobbed her mother, starting to slur her words. "Edna's daughters are taking care of all the details and I'm going to fit in her customers too until the end of the week. After that I don't know," she sobbed.

A Message from Katrina

"Do you want me to come over?" Coli asked in a cowardly fashion.

"No," said her mother. "I'll be fine." She quickly hung up the phone, which Coli took to mean that more than one bottle had been opened and Charlene didn't want any disapproving company. Coli thought to herself: a better daughter than I am would have gone over anyways. She sighed and thought, I just can't face it.

Coli looked at the clock. Orlando was probably already at the River Daze. She suddenly couldn't face that either. She slumped onto her couch for a while and then wandered aimlessly around the apartment. Finally, the groceries spilling out of the bag by the door impinged on her grief. She pulled herself together enough to put them away and briefly considered making herself a meal. Her appetite seemed to be gone. She settled for a quiet evening of remembering and grieving for a woman who had been a good friend to a young girl.

The music swirled around Coli, as she nursed her beer and tapped her feet to the feel and sway of the jazz. She was tired but glad to be here on a Friday night. Orlando had left her a message at work, asking her to come to the River Daze tonight. She thought he had said something about "as close as he could come to a date", but she still didn't know how to interpret that. She watched him with pleasure. He seemed to be putting himself, body and soul, into the music. What an appealing body too! Thoughts and feelings that she hadn't thought or felt in a long while started to circulate through her.

Suddenly, she realized that the set had ended and that Orlando was getting up from the piano. He did his usual slow stroll through the tables and his conversations with friends. She wondered if his slow progress to her dark and shadowed corner was a deliberate tease or just low-key friendliness.

Finally, he reached across the table and gave her a hug. "It's good to see your face…. And certainly the rest of you. How y'all been? I've missed you," he said with a rush of feeling that made Coli giddy. I am seriously losing it, she thought.

Embarrassed by her reaction, Coli muttered something about being busy at work and then blurted out, "Edna died. You know Edna? She worked with my Mama for years. She was a good friend to me. Quiet, always quiet, but she knew what was going on with me and was pretty good at deflecting my mom's criticism without getting her back up. Well, she died."

Orlando slid onto the bench seat behind the table and gathered Coli into him. She laid her head against his shoulder but couldn't stop herself from continuing. "I was late for the funeral, which annoyed my mother. I spent most of the service blubbering into a tissue, which annoyed my mother. I left the reception early, which really annoyed my mother. But I had to go back to the station to finish a public information segment about how to be prepared for this storm that might be building up in the Gulf." Coli managed to put the brakes on her mouth, but feared that she had already passed the hysterical female parameters.

Orlando was quietly stroking her arm to the rhythm of the new group. He said, "Try to relax for a bit. This group is almost as good as we are."

"You are so good at this."

"What?"

"Listening"

"Pure survival!"

"You have a lot of girlfriends who foam at the mouth?"

"No, sisters. Don't you remember my four older sisters?" Coli didn't, not really. She had a vague memory of Orlando's sisters being quite a bit older than he was. She hadn't really sorted them out as a child and had never considered the implications of living in a household with four older sisters.

Orlando continued, "My mama, Jeanne, is still running her catering business. My two older sisters are working with her. When they were younger, Marie, Hélène,

Lucie, and Thérèse could really get going at times. I know more about make-up and women's fashions than any self-respecting male ought to. As I got older I learned how to shut the talk out. Practicing on the sax or the piano was a good way to avoid the longest of their discussions.

"Sometimes I did listen. I do like to listen to other people. I learn a lot. I've never really learned much from books. It's always sort of been people and music for me." He smiled at Coli and hugged her again.

They listened in silence to the music while Coli recovered. Orlando kissed her behind the ear and said, "My last set. Why don't you stay and I'll take you home after."

That helped Coli recover. She murmured, "Good idea. I thought you'd never suggest it."

Coli opened one eye and squinted at the clock. It was too early on Saturday morning, but if she wanted to make breakfast for the two of them, before she headed back to work to help keep the free world safe from storms, she'd better move her butt. So thinking, she wiggled it a little, and snuggled right up to Orlando's back.

Ah, the pleasures of loving a good, vibrant and patient man. Various parts of her body tingled at the thought of the time they had spent together during the night.

The phone's shrill ring interrupted her thoughts. She leaped out of bed thinking that her mother must be truly pissed if she was phoning this early to harass her. Her surprise was complete when her boss, George, answered her hesitant, "Hello?"

"Sorry to phone so early," his gravelly voice reached out. "I've just been called by B A NEWS. They want to 'borrow' you for a few days to provide local knowledge and colour for their coverage of the storm, if it continues to brew. Naturally, I told them that you were too busy putting together a storm preparedness broadcast to waste time with them."

Coli was slow to make sense of what he said. B A NEWS! At College most of her friends referred to the network as BAN as in 'BAN the truth' by selective reporting. Other students said it put a BANd-aid on some of the wounds of mankind but didn't even notice others that were bleeding the body 'politique' dry. Once they were through being smart-ass college kids, absolutely nobody on the college newspaper team, not even the most radical, could pretend that Best American News wasn't the only game in the country for a serious career. Coli Duncan, a household name! Her dearly held ambition reasserted itself.

"Of course, I'm just kidding. Coli, you still there? Coli?"

"I'm here. I'm here", she replied when she could make her mouth work again.

"You need to get down here right away. We have to decide how you can go to work for them for the storm and send some of your stuff to us."

"I'm coming as soon as I can," she said and dropped the phone down without even noticing it. She swirled around in delight to see Orlando rubbing his eyes and looking at her.

"I've got to catch a shower and then scoot down to work for a bit. BAN the truth wants to hire me! I've arrived! I'll be able to afford a car, maybe a used Escort, or if the storm goes on long enough, a new Ford." Coli grabbed her underwear and lunged into the bathroom while avoiding direct eye contact with Orlando.

A few minutes later she streaked into the room and threw on her clothes. She combed her hair and looked for Orlando. Not still in the bed. Maybe he'd left already. Part of her felt guilty. Part of her said "good" because she was ashamed at leaving him like this. Another part of her quivered, scared, in an emotional corner, saying 'good-bye' to a wonderful relationship that had just been beginning. She scooped up her backpack and hurried for the door.

A Message from Katrina

She came around the corner of the hall and ran right into Orlando who was leaning against the door, his arms folded across his chest. "You don't get rid of me this easy" he said through gritted teeth. "I'm not interested in a one-night stand, Coli".

"Neither am I", replied Coli, "but I've got to go. My whole future depends on it."

"Not your whole future, only your job," he said slowly.

That checked Coli's headlong flight, but not for long. "Forgive me. I loved the time we spent together. See you very soon," she pleaded as she eased by him to the outside hallway.

"I'm going to Grand Falls," she heard him call after her.

Orlando grimaced at his bloodshot eyes and hair clumped here and there. If this was what one night with Coli did to him, he might have to re-adjust his daydreams. He threw water at his face and rubbed it out of his eyes. He was so angry he started to mutter out loud.

"Yah, right. If I ever see her again. Right. Good move, Romeo. Tell her in the morning." He ran his hands through his hair in an attempt at control. "Your great news. What a sucker. Save every penny for years for a down payment on a broken down warehouse in a dying town. Owner, operator, musician of your own club in the middle of nowhere. Yah, she'll really want to be part of that." He pulled his t-shirt over his head and got ready to leave Coli's apartment.

CHAPTER 8

DREAMS COME TRUE

Coli came puffing in the door just as George was heading out with his arms around a box. "Wow, the bus was late. It seems like everyone is on the move. Maybe we won't need to rebroadcast the Emergency Preparedness Information if everyone is leaving the city," she called out to his retreating back. Inside, the more delicate parts of their operation were already packed up, rejected tapes and discs piled on her desk.

George reappeared at her office door. He said, "The Mayor and the Governor are both calling for evacuation. The mayor has been quoted as saying: 'We're facing the storm most of us have feared.' The weather service is calling for winds reaching 175 m.p.h., which makes this storm a Category 5 Hurricane. Right now it's headed straight for us. Worse yet, some of the city engineers are saying that the storm surge could overtop some of the levees."*

"So this means that you are not going to be here, manning the station in our hour of need?"

"Don't confuse heroism with stupidity, Coli. Electronics don't mix with water, fire, or extreme wind," he retorted as he stuffed parts of her computer and miles of cords into a box. "Pack up as much small valuable stuff as you can. I took us off the air twenty minutes ago and told our valued viewers to tune in to Best American News for as long as they were able to. I can only fill up half the van. My wife is insisting on filling the rest with life support."

"Life support?" echoed Coli.

"Yeah, you know. Food, clothing, bedding, money and sports mags."

"I thought you had planned to stick it out. My mother plans to stay here, like always."

"This one could be the big one. Besides, the wife has talked a lot about retiring. We were thinking about Florida, but it had four evacuations last hurricane season, so we thought we'd stay here. Now, our very nice place in Lakeview is looking a little less attractive."

"Your place does look up to the beauty of Lake Pontchartrain," Coli offered.

"Smart comments don't help real estate values," George grunted as he hefted another overflowing cardboard box. "Keep packing," he tossed over his shoulder as he made another trip to the van.

A Message from Katrina

They packed as quickly as they could while the heat and humidity mounted. If they hadn't believed in the modern science of meteorology they couldn't have conceived that a storm was coming. It seemed like a normal, sunny, hot, and sweaty late August day. Finally, slightly more than half of the van was filled. They started locking up what was left. Coli couldn't wait any longer. She asked George, "Where are you heading for?"

"Grand Falls."

"Grand Falls?" echoed Coli.

"Why are you so surprised?" George questioned. "You've been there. It's far enough away from the city. It's on slightly higher ground and the town is in a bit of a valley so it will have some shelter from the wind. Plus, we've got reservations at the Campground."

"You and half of New Orleans," snorted Coli.

"You have a better plan?"

"I've got a job. You promised me details if I helped with the packing."

"You're working with Roger Silverfox". Coli clutched her heart and did a dramatic swoon. "Don't mock. He's one of the best and you're lucky to be in the right place at the right time and at the right age."

"I'll get out my violin, George." Coli teased.

"Ingratitude, thou marble hearted fiend,/ More hideous when thou show'st thee in a child"*, quoted George as he surged by with one more box.

There he goes again, thought Coli. It just reeked of Shakespeare but she couldn't quite place the quote. Hours in the lecture hall wasted.

"Why did I get this job?" Coli suddenly thought to ask.

George looked uncomfortable. "You know. Young, keen, sweet face. Why not?"

"Right. Not my great abilities then. Friends who know friends who know friends."

"You should be grateful," he snorted. "Showtime now. No more moaning about how you only need a chance to show how great you are."

"Yeah, I'm grateful but it seemed to come out of nowhere, just like this storm. This storm that is getting closer, boss".

"Ex-boss," he replied. "Silverfox will go to your apartment and pick you up when he arrives with his equipment van this afternoon. You need whatever city maps and other notes you have to get around. Especially maps with elevations above sea level and other useful details. Whatever personal stuff you need and your video-cam. You'll be staying at The Grand because it's in the French Quarter, which is, of course, on higher ground. It is also one of the few hotels with a corporate housed server in Dallas so it should continue to have Internet possibilities if the local connections go down."

"Silverfox tell you all this?" asked Coli.

"Yeah, he said that the network van could feed into a satellite relay system for as long as he had enough fuel to power his generator. So you two should be able to get the news out. Good-luck. Come and see me in Grand Falls when you can," he offered.

"George, I really do want to thank you for this chance. And, well, Roger Silverfox has been an idol of mine for years, so this is like, wow, really exciting." Coli rushed toward him and gave him a tentative hug. He returned a bear hug and drove off in the van before she could recover from her surprise.

Coli felt like crawling up the stairs to her apartment. The bus and walking patchwork she had created to get home had drained her energy. All of the traffic was headed in one direction and she was struggling to go in the other. Last minute shopping had been done in a frenzy of near panic by those not leaving and actual panic by those trying to get out of town. Some stores were already closed. Others were in the process of being boarded up. When she had been forced to detour through the Garden District in her bus odyssey she had seen the windows being boarded up in the fine old houses. Everybody seemed to have too little time to do what needed to be done.

Including herself. At least there was no Best America News van parked outside her apartment yet. She huffed up the stairs and struggled with the lock. Inside, all was as it had been this morning. This morning seemed like it had happened in another dimension. She would phone Orlando while she ate as much as she could. You never knew if meals would be regular over the next few days.

Coli tried Orlando's number. No answer. She set the phone on redial and started to eat the edibles in her fridge and throw out the 'best before' items. She thought that she must remember to get the garbage down the chute before she left. Still no answer. She started to load up her largest wheeled suitcase—maps, notes, meds, cans of sardines, tuna, and ravioli, energy bars, six bottled water and her least wrinkled, best clothes. She was going to be on TV. She would be a household name. Thank-you Katrina. Still no answer.

Maybe she had to give up on Orlando. Her heart gave a little lurch but the excitement for her grand adventure shoved that feeling out of the way. She thought of the storm: high winds and brave deeds bringing the viewing public the inside story, storm surges and overtopped levees. This would give great ratings. Whoa, back up that train of thought—levees, storm surges, Lower Ninth Ward, Reverend Weekes, levees repairs ignored, her mama's house, her mama in her trailer riding out the storm.

She punched the numbers on her phone with trembling fingers. The phone was picked up on the second ring. "Mama?"

"That you, Coli?" Her mother's annoyed tone and slightly slurred words came at her.

"I was hoping you would have evacuated by now."

"Evacuated? Why? We rode out lots of storms right in this here trailer when you were growing up," her mother replied belligerently.

Coli remembered every minute of every one of them: the shrieking of the wind and sometimes her mother. Other times her mother was passed out on the bed and she was crouched in the corner of her mama's closet. She would put her hands over her ears, make herself as small as possible and pray to God. She made all kinds of promises to God if only He would stop the storm and the ear-splitting sound of the wind. One good storm produced months of church attendance, she remembered. Coli suddenly realized that her mother was probably as terrified as she was but dealt with it differently. Funny, that had never occurred to her before.

"Mama, I've been hired by Best American News to provide local knowledge to Roger Silverfox's coverage of hurricane Katrina here in New Orleans. I'm going to be famous."

"My daughter, a household name," Charlene drawled.

Why did she still keep hoping that her mother would be excited for her? She should know by now how sarcastic her mother became after a few beers.

"Well, I hope you're happy. I hope the storm and all the destruction will make good TV ratings. Too bad TVs here won't be working."

Coli reined in her anger one more time. "You're right. The storm probably will knock out the power. I really think you ought to leave this time," Coli urged, glancing one more time at her TV screen. "The B A News coverage is calling it a monster hurricane."

"You're as bad as Stella. She was just here from next-door, pounding on my door. She says that Reverend Weekes has organized some more busses to take everyone in the Parish to Grand Falls. What a stupid idea! I've got my supplies in and I'm staying right here. Famous, hah!" Her mother slammed down the receiver.

Coli was punching her mother's phone number to try again when she heard the buzz from her door. Whirling around, she hit the intercom button. She heard, "Roger Silverfox here". "Come right up," she managed to say as her excitement started to build.

A Message from Katrina

After slamming down the phone, Charlene looked at it in anger. Run from a storm? Not her, she'd been facing them down for years. She remembered her terror as a child. She could still hear the shrieking wind, the walls of the house trembling as another storm hit the bayou. More than once, her family had lost some of the roof. She remembered cowering right here, in this trailer, looking after Coli, trying to comfort her as a child. She had shuddered as much as the trailer at every blast of wind.

She looked at her beer can as she reached for it. Yeah, maybe she had tried to block it out a bit, just a bit. Yeah, well Coli wasn't a baby anymore so she didn't have to worry about her and the TV had gone on and on about this being a monster storm. She heaved herself to her feet and shuffled down to the bedroom.

She started to dig around in the back of her closet. She pulled out clothes that had been lost for some time and some others that she had never really liked all that much. Finally she found a scruffy, old and wrinkled duffle bag. She should have realized that Ed wasn't coming back when he had bought a new suitcase, instead of taking his duffle bag.

She waited for the pain to come, the pain and sadness. She had felt that her life was over without him and yet she still had Coli to look after. No feeling came to her, except a vague annoyance that the duffle bag looked so beat up and she really didn't have anything else. Twenty years was probably long enough to grieve a first love. She wasn't that teenager any more. Even Coli was older than she had been at the time.

Her mind faded out for a time. She came back to herself and started to shove in clothes, toothpaste, brushes. She heard someone pounding on the door. Probably that bloody Stella she thought as she shuffled toward the noise.

CHAPTER 9

CLAY FEET

Coli raced with her garbage along the hallway to the chute. She ran back to her apartment and headed for the window. Grabbing the bent barbecue fork from behind the curtains, and reaching for the window, she opened it and hooked the fork onto the wrought iron bolts. Using all her strength she pulled and finally swung the heavy wooden shutters over the window. Storms had been pounding this city for a long time. That had been smart, spending an afternoon with WD40 patiently lubricating the shutter's moving bits. The bolt screeched into place. Oops, a bit more needed there.

Roger was knocking on the door by the time she spun around. She opened it quickly and stepped back a pace. He was even better looking in real life than on the screen. How amazing! He was tall and still slim. Grey was creeping into his thick, black hair, making him look even stronger and more trustworthy. High cheekbones from his

Cherokee grandmother and a lanky, muscular height from some Scot's ancestor created that well-known media package. Wow! thought Coli. Finally, I am getting to meet the man himself, the person behind that confident and knowledgeable image. Wow!

"Coli Duncan, I presume," he drawled. His intense black eyes focused on her glowing face. The slight sneer in his voice promised a bad beginning but he had been traveling all day and maybe she didn't look better in real life. All right, she knew she was a little too short and a little too curvy to fit with all those meat-skewer shaped women on TV. She pasted a smile on her face and said sweetly, "Hi, I'm ready if you are. I've lived through a lot of storms here but this could really be 'the storm of the century'." She hefted her backpack, and her camera. Then she started towing her suitcase. Apparently oblivious to her attempt at collegiality, Roger glanced at her suitcase in amazement.

"You're taking all that?"

"Only as far as the hotel," answered Coli. "Show me the best way to get there," was all that Roger said as they headed for the stairs. "The way I took to get here was not the best but, at least, most of the traffic was heading in the other direction."

A Message from Katrina

The route that Coli had planned was the most efficient on paper and based on day-to-day traffic. However, today was not a normal day and traffic was bottlenecked on any route leading out of town. Hot and annoyed, they finally arrived in the hotel lobby. Roger said, "Register under B A News. I'll meet you in the lobby in fifteen minutes. Don't keep me waiting." Not exactly as warm and friendly as he appeared in front of the camera, Coli thought as she struggled toward the desk.

She was back in the lobby, ready for work with her mini-cam and necessary bits in her backpack fourteen minutes later. She looked smugly around the lobby, but didn't see Roger. She checked her watch. Finally, she saw him coming toward her carrying the latest compact digital video camera. He came nearer and peered at her camera closely. "I didn't think anyone even had one of those any more, let alone used it for news coverage." Coli could feel her cheeks getting red. Roger didn't seem to notice.

"Come on", he flung at her over his shoulder. "I asked at the desk how to get up to the roof for the best view."

Coli looked all around herself in wonder. She could see for miles from up here. The trip up the service staircase and a little used, narrow corridor had been worth it. At least Roger knew how to find a compelling vantage point to launch his commentary.

The hot summer sun poured over an amazing scene. She could see two of the main routes out of town. Both of them involved long bridges and even longer lines of cars, most of which were not moving. A swaying pall of exhaust fumes shimmered over the vehicles. Tiny ant-like people were scurrying around. Other people were inside their cars, resigned to the wait, or else furious. Either way, not much was moving. The lanes coming into town were now empty, except for police and fire department vehicles.

The whole city had a surreal look to it. Light was flashing from the car windows or mirrors; trees and houses shimmered in the heat. The colours were there but the normal sounds were much muted, as if the city held its breath in fear and wonder.

Coli was getting some of it on her camera, but Roger was panning the scene with purpose. He stopped from time to time for the names of streets or districts, which Coli supplied. Most, she knew. For a few, she had to put down her camera and scrabble through her maps. Suddenly, she caught a bright flare of light from down on the highway. A boom of sound quickly followed it. She and Roger turned towards the sound and light, just in time to catch the flare and sound of three other explosions.

"Can you get us there?" Roger called out as he stuffed everything into his pack.

A Message from Katrina

"We can get close on a road that doesn't cross the highway, but we'll have to walk in for the last few hundred feet," Coli replied, as she slung her camera and pack over her shoulder.

The traffic had been massively lopsided as Coli picked out the most passable streets. No one wanted to be on a street that didn't get onto the I-10 right now. Finally, they were up against the barrier and trudging up a trail worn smooth by the footsteps of many local people. They came up near the fire and saw a scene of devastation. They could just make out the name RESTHAVEN—Security for Sen—on the side of the remains of a burning bus.

"Ten minutes, Coli. I'll interview while you run the mini-cam and then you interview while I run the camera. Let's get the news out." Roger hurried over to a burly guy near the front door of the bus.

Coli was so excited that she could barely breathe. This was the big time! Don't blow it now, she told herself. She looked around through the curtains of smoke. Bodies lay on the roadway, between and against cars. Cars closest to the wrecked bus were abandoned. Their passengers were huddled together near the edge of the road, three lanes away. Coli hoped there wouldn't be any more explosions.

She could feel her stomach curling in on itself in excitement and fear. She hoped she wouldn't faint.

Roger looked over his shoulder and shouted at her, "Move it. This isn't a meditation exercise."

Coli started to get her camera out as she ran nearer to Roger and the bus. She stopped near him and panned the burning bus. She focused on Roger's face and then on the burly bus driver who stumbled out of the bus, with an old man draped over his shoulder.

Roger shoved his mike in the man's face. "What just happened here?"

The guy looked at him in amazement and shouted, "Can't you see? The bus exploded."

"Why?"

"I don't know. Maybe a spark connected with the oxygen tank of one of the patients in the back. Gimme a hand here. Lots of old folks need help in there."

"I'm a reporter," Roger replied.

"Then get out of my way," shouted the bus driver as he shoved Roger out of the way and hurried away from the burning bus with his burden. Coli got ready to drop her camera and rush into the bus. She realized that the sirens she had been hearing for the last few minutes were almost on top of her. The blinking lights were affecting her vision. The headache starting up was not helping her stomach or her incipient dizziness.

A Message from Katrina

Roger shouted at her, "Your turn." He started to grab his camera and looked to her for direction. She saw two people huddled on the pavement on the far side of a car, sheltered from the worst of the burning bus.

"Over there," she shouted and started towards them. One woman, with blood flowing down her arm, was bending over some one else. She tried to inject seriousness into her voice to cover up her excitement.

"Hi, I'm Coli Duncan from Best American News," she said as she poked her ID badge into the woman's face. "Can you tell me what happened here?"

The woman looked at her in a dazed fashion. "Reporter?" she croaked. "I need a medic here!" She continued to hold the sleeve of her shirt pressed tightly against the forehead of the older woman on the ground.

"Someone's on the way," said Coli as she tuned into the wail of emergency vehicles again. "What happened?" Coli continued to prod a response from her.

"I don't know," she replied slowly. "I'm a nurse at Resthaven. When the evacuation order came, we took everyone in the bus, but we didn't think we'd be packed on the highway like sardines. Maybe there was a spark from the brakes or something else. We may have had a leak in one of the oxygen lines for our inhalers. I don't know.

"When I heard the explosion at the back of the bus, I helped Jean out as quickly as I could. The second explosion hit us outside the bus. I was hit in the arm and she stumbled and fell. She cut her forehead. She's still unconscious." The nurse seemed to have wound down in her story. She continued to press on the wound and stare fixedly at the ground.

Coli felt that she needed to do something to help. She turned around to survey the others who were injured. She stood up just as Roger touched her arm. "Time's up," he said. "Let's get this out to the viewing public".

"But shouldn't we help until the medics arrive?" asked Coli.

Roger looked at her with exasperation. "We're not the nuns of Nicaragua sustaining the hopeless," he sneered. "We're reporters covering the greatest natural disaster of our careers. Now. Come on. Time's up. Let's go."

They struggled back to the van as quickly as they could. Roger unlocked the back and swung up into its crowded interior. "Come on. Give me your camera." He reached for it as he shooed her away. "Let's see if you've got anything worth sending," he smirked as he reached for her camera pack.

"I'll help", said Coli, even though she felt breathless and her head was starting to swim.

"No, you go up front and wait until I'm finished. It's too crowded for both of us in here and you don't look so good."

A Message from Katrina

Between the aerial views from the hotel roof and the two interviews at the burning bus, Roger put together a five-minute sight and sound byte. It gave the viewers a good sense of what was happening, at Ground Zero, in New Orleans, on the eve of perhaps the biggest storm of the century. They drove back to the hotel in exhausted silence. Coli wasn't thinking or feeling anymore. The trip back was just a blank of shock.

In the large downstairs lobby was a group of all those who couldn't or wouldn't leave town. Phoning a taxi was of absolutely no use right now. It was eerily quiet as all eyes were glued to a large TV set up in the corner of the room. The weather channel had become an all time favourite. Swirling spirals of bright colours moved around the screen as an earnest voice said, "Landfall is expected near New Orleans at about 6:00 am. Winds are predicted to reach 175 m.p.h. Some officials fear that Katrina's storm surge could overtop New Orleans' levees."*

"And now our first report from our man at Ground Zero, Roger Silverfox." The scene changed to a slow pan of the city from a high point, undoubtedly the roof of the hotel. The lines of cars were zoomed into the forefront. Roger's smooth voice gave the commentary. "Here we are in New Orleans, just before the arrival of the biggest hurricane of the 21st century. Lanes leading into the city are now closed to all except emergency vehicles. There has been talk of setting up a counterflow in these lanes, but nothing has happened yet. As you can see, outgoing lanes are completely motionless."

Suddenly, the bang of the first explosion was heard and the camera swung to catch the next explosions and bursts of flame. Then, there was a quick change to Roger interviewing the bus driver. As the bus driver came out of the bus, carrying the old man, she heard Roger ask him: "What just happened here?"

Coli heard the bus driver's angry voice, "Can't you see? The bus is exploding."

"Why?"

"I don't know. Maybe the spark connected with the oxygen tanks of one of the patients at the back." Coli expected to hear the bus driver go on and ask for their help, but instead Roger panned to the emergency vehicles. He did a voice over, "Fortunately, ambulance and firetrucks are on the scene." He looked concerned and somehow gave the impression that he had solved the problem. Coli felt herself feeling safe, as she always did watching Roger Silverfox report a harrowing incident on TV. Coli admired his skill at the same time that she realized that perhaps the real Roger was not quite as caring as he appeared on TV.

Then, he made a quick segue into her interview with the nurse and the unconscious patient. The viewing public was treated to the side of Coli's face and a microphone stretched out to the nurse. Coli heard the nurse saying: "When the evacuation order came we took everyone in the bus. We didn't think we'd be packed on the highway like sardines. Maybe there was a spark from the brakes or something else." As Coli watched the interview she was amazed at how professional she looked. She felt a quick burst of pride. She was a B A News reporter. She was on her way!

Roger turned to Coli. "Well, that'll give them something to play while we catch some sleep. If we want to report the landfall we'll need to meet here at 4:00 am. Think of a hotel near the water that will give us some shelter and a good view of the action. If we get the van close enough we can set up a live feed of the storm."

"What happens if the storm comes in faster and we miss it?" asked Coli anxiously. Roger looked at her as if she were too stupid for words.

"I'm going to leave a request at the front desk. If there's any immediate action they'll call me. Believe me, when the action starts you won't be sleeping for a long time."

Although exhausted, Coli knew that she couldn't possibly sleep after all the excitement. Her headache had not gone away yet and moving too quickly made her feel dizzy. She also needed a shower. She could smell the sweat and fear on her body and her clothes.

Despite the shower she still felt agitated as she climbed into the strange bed. The wind was gusting outside the hotel and the rain was beginning to patter on the window. Even here on the lee side of the hotel the winds were starting to sound like the roar of an approaching train. She'd better take some meds before her headache became a pounding migraine, too often induced by the low pressure preceding most hurricanes. Hurricane Katrina sure seemed more of a reality now than it had this afternoon under the sunny skies and the heat of one more summer day.

She found her meds and took them, hoping to avoid the worst of the coming migraine. She snuggled into the luxury of a hotel bed and tried to will herself to sleep. She was exhausted but her mind just wouldn't shut down. Gotta sleep. Can't sleep. She saw the burning bus in her mind's eye. How mad the bus driver had been. None of that appeared in the news. Everyone pitched in to help empty the bus. Yeah, everyone who was there, after Media Star Roger Silverfox left to get the news out.

Stop, stop, she told herself. Gotta sleep. Can't sleep. The noise of the wind, the force of it pounded in her head. Stop, stop. Gotta sleep. Can't sleep. It seemed impossible that just twenty-four hours ago she had been curled up with Orlando, thinking of him. Thinking of finding more time to spend with him. She hoped he had got safely out of town, maybe with his family in that bus to Grand Falls. Wow, would it ever be crowded. Stop, stop. Gotta sleep. Can't sleep. Gotta sleep. Can't sleep. In mid-thought she fell into a deep, black hole.

CHAPTER 10

A DANCE WITH THE DEVIL

No time seemed to have passed when she heard a persistent buzzing. Her muzzy brain finally identified it as an alarm clock. Her head was throbbing from the storm migraine. At least her meds kept the pain to a dull throb. She could still function if she really concentrated. Three thirty a.m. She'd better get moving. She wouldn't put it past Roger to strike out on his own and grab all the glory. She crawled out of bed and started putting on her most glamorous, tough- weather clothes. The electricity was still working so she made herself some coffee and opened a tin of tuna. The power would suddenly go down at some point in the storm. With the wind pounding like a freight train out there she was surprised that it hadn't already happened.

When she reached the lobby, she realized that the big windows had been boarded up while she slept. There was a huddle of people in front of the TV. Roger was among them. They had their attention riveted on Katrina Advisory No.25, issued by the National Hurricane Centre in Miami just a few minutes ago. The words were chilling: "…areas affected by the storm will be uninhabitable for weeks…over half of homes and most of industrial buildings will be nonfunctional…concrete block apartments will sustain major damage and wood frame buildings will be destroyed. All living persons and animals in the area must remain indoors. Winds will be full of light and heavy airborne debris such as household appliances and even small vehicles. Power outages will last for weeks and there will be water shortages. If you are still in the affected areas fill all suitable containers with drinking water now and remain indoors. This advisory will be updated on the half-hour."

Coli looked at Roger and hurried back to her room. She filled everything that would hold water, including the tub and sink. The water pressure seemed low, so she knew she wasn't the only person heeding the warning.

When she returned to the lobby she saw Roger in a serious conversation with a lanky young guy in a security uniform. On seeing her he broke off the conversation and hurried over. Coli said, "Are we going out in that?" She could hear the wind banging things against the plywood on the windows.

"Don't confuse dedication to duty with stupidity, Coli. I just talked to Jerry, the security guard. We'll watch their cams on the parking lot until the main winds pass by and then we'll go out and see the damage."

They turned and followed Jerry through a labyrinth of hallways to the tiny office. Three of the cams faced outside to the open. They turned their attention to the storm scenes recorded there. The air was full of paper and plastic of all sizes and colours. Tree branches and leaves fluttered past the front of the cameras. A table leg whirled by and a toaster rolled and fell in the gusts of wind. A shopping cart twirled across the parking lot. Then they heard the shattering of glass and one of the cams went blank.

They watched the other two, constantly amazed by what went by: tools, books, photos partly ripped out of broken frames, clothing bits and more than one shoe. Finally, the other two cams were also broken by the flying debris, and they were left with only dull thuds and the shriek of the wind for company.

"Jerry," said Roger, "I'll take the disks and edit them for my news update. I'll have them back to you very soon. Coli, you see what food you can find. We'll eat up and then, as soon as the wind drops enough to get out, we'll go looking for what's news worthy."

A Message from Katrina

Roger had to hand it to Coli. She sure did know how to pick 'em. This hotel would give them a better overview of the storm near the water. Once the wind had dropped enough they had been able to drive, at a bit better than a walking pace, around several detours of downed trees and building debris. They were now holed up in the new hotel's lobby, close to his van outside in the parking lot. It was near enough for the necessary electrical lines to snake their way to the extra lights that could be carried out the door and around the building.

He could hear the howling of the storm winds out there. The parking lot sloped down to the water that seemed to be rising at an alarming rate. His lights clearly showed the fury of raindrops pelting against everything in sight. It was still a mother of a storm.

"I'm ready." Roger looked around to see Coli in the cocoon of a new slicker, glaringly yellow in the bright light. Roger took the camera and she adjusted her microphone so it would clearly transmit and yet be protected from the force of the wind. She said as she rounded the corner, "Winds are starting to slacken off here from earlier peak gusts. It is still hard to walk against them."

She staggered visibly as a gust lifted her up for a second. "Branches are being broken from trees." The noise of small thumps and bangs was continuous. "Abandoned coffee cups, papers, and plastic bags are swirling around in the air like modern dervishes. Part of the plastic hotel sign has broken and is hitting the main sign with every severe gust of wind." All of her commentary was accompanied by clever camera shots from Roger, which would be beamed up to the satellite and give every viewer a ringside, yet safe look, at the unfolding catastrophe. "This is Coli Duncan at the Riverside Hotel, New Orleans, signing off.".

"Whoa! Did you see that, Roger? I was just about blown off my feet by that gust near the end," enthused Coli.

"Nerves of steel from our cub reporter", replied Roger sourly.

"Are you just naturally miserable or do you have to work at it, Roger?" asked Coli in exasperation. It had already been a long morning and she was getting a little tired of Roger and his comments, especially when she considered her misplaced hero worship. He sure kept his calm and understanding image for the viewing public.

She started to walk closer to the building where she would be more sheltered from the wind. She heard Roger shout, "Look out!" She turned her head to see what the problem was…

A Message from Katrina

She looked into Roger's face. He was lifting up a bandage that was wound around her forehead. Her headache had morphed into a pounding rock band located just behind her eyes. "Not to worry. Just a glancing blow from a bit of debris. The bleeding's stopped. Just stay here for a minute while I send out what we already filmed. You'll be better soon." While he wasn't exactly Florence Nightengale, Coli could already feel the pounding beat of her headache slowing down. She didn't feel well enough to move from the back of the van yet but she would force herself to move soon.

The next time, Roger ventured out into the wind and she filmed. They found out later that landfall had been at Buras, a bayou town about 70 miles southeast of New Orleans. The first photos in showed that the town had been completely destroyed.

The destruction was bad enough where they were. At the height of the wind and rain the hotel sign had come loose and crashed into the pole. Then it had hit three different cars in the lot, and finally hammered itself against the side of the wine and beer store beside the hotel. All of this was sent out live to millions of TV viewers who cringed in their armchairs from the force of the storm. One unforgettable series of shots showed the water level in the parking lot rising over the course of four hours until finally two of the smaller cars in the lot rose with it and slowly sailed across the lot.   In slow motion they gracefully scraped and rebounded off other cars and posts.   Their actions seemed unrelated to the insurance claims and the auto-body repairs that surely lay ahead in their murky futures.

The rain was still pounding down, but less furiously. The wind was still blowing but not shrieking when Roger decided that it was time to troll any streets they could get through on their return to the hotel. The trip back was perilous and slow. Trees were down on some of the roads. Wires were strewn across other streets.   Some areas were flooded.   Their route back was long and frequently trailed back on itself, but they did find some action.

Roger suddenly called out, "Look, Coli! Looters!" He wheeled over to the side of the road and dashed into a convenience store, past the broken glass in the windows and the door ripped off its hinges. Several guys in dirty T-shirts, stained shorts and wet boots looked up in surprise. The tallest one, with tattoos running down both arms, said, "We're helpin' Henri clean up.   He's gonna need to be ready soon when people can get out and around.   You wanna help too?"

"No," replied Roger, clearly disappointed.

The other guys all stopped their cleaning and started to loom over Roger. He looked around and said, "Who's Henri?"

"Right here, man."

"Coli and I would like to buy fifty dollars worth of your stock, if you're willing to let it go," he added. Getting a nod, he continued, "Coli, you pick it out while I decide where we're going next." He walked out confidently and climbed into his van. Coli climbed in slowly a few minutes later with a fairly small bag.

"Looters," she snorted. "Local entrepreneurs more like." Seeing Roger's look of disdain at her bag she continued, "Prices are only going to rise." She settled herself in the passenger seat. She tried to ignore it but her head still hurt.

They continued on past houses missing roofs and walls. Looking in, Coli could see the remains of personal lives. The sheer scope of the disaster started to weigh on her. She kept seeing the burning bus in her mind's eye. They came around one corner and saw the wall of a mausoleum ripped right out. Urns and caskets were scattered on the ground. No one seemed to be back yet to deal with the desecration.

They decided to head over to Lake Pontchartrain to see if damage had been bad in the Garden District in some of the heritage residences. They were surprised to see an old man smoking a cigarette and rocking in his chair on the front porch of an antebellum home that appeared to have suffered no significant damage. Coli said, "Stop, Roger. I want to talk to him."

Roger rolled his eyes but he did pull over.

Coli struggled out of the van. She was really beginning to feel her early morning and her head still hurt. Her eyes were feeling sore and gummy. She rubbed them and realized her fingers were dirty too. She almost fell over a branch on the sidewalk. She stopped to get her balance and took a good look at the house. It was centered on a small knoll, in the lee of a slightly higher hill. It looked like a small scale plantation house built before the Civil War. The white painted siding had been ripped off in places and one of the shutters was hanging by its last hinge. Oak tree branches littered the lawn and one old tree had crashed down just feet from the front porch. Broken branches littered the porch steps.

"Hi, I'm Coli Duncan from B A News. I'm a little surprised to see you here."

"George Scheffler," he said as he shook her hand. "Shouldn't be surprised. I've been right here through every hurricane for the last seventy-five years."

"Your house doesn't seem to have been seriously damaged."

"It was made when places were built to last and owners could choose the exact best place to build."

"Aren't you afraid of looters?" Coli asked.

"Nope, neighbours are pretty good at helping out in bad times," he replied.

Coli could see Roger motioning from the van. "Thanks very much for your time," she finished up and turned to leave.

"Let's go," said Roger. "I want to see this lake that's higher than the surrounding neighbourhood."

"Levees are really important around here, Roger. In fact, just a while ago I interviewed Rev. Weekes who had set up a media event to show everybody how high the water would get if the levees broke."

"And?" He prompted.

"In some areas it would be up to the first floor or roof tops."

"But, that hasn't happened, has it?"

"Probably not. Probably the water we've seen in low lying areas is from the rain and the remains of the storm surge that came in with landfall and high tide."

"I hope you're right. Is that the lake behind that levee over there?"

"Yes, it is." Coli turned to look at the levee. "Roger, we have to get out of here right now! Turn the van around right now!"

"Why? I want to get closer and see about that little trickle coming over that section. See it over there? That'll make good footage"

"No! Turn around right now! Dedication to duty is not the same as stupidity. That trickle should not be there and it could very soon be more than a trickle. See how high that levee is and how low we are? Now turn around right now!"

Roger could hear the fear in Coli's voice. He decided that since the local journalist always knows, he'd better do a quick u-turn. They left as soon as he could turn around and headed for higher ground past the continuing litter of houses and trees. Roger stopped the van. He climbed out with his camera and put on more lenses. He turned to Coli who was hugging her elbows while a niggling of anxiety grew. "Now, be ready to give our viewers the salient details while I pan the scene of the leak." He moved the camera slowly and carefully. "As you have seen, damage from winds and rain has been extensive. However, a new danger is becoming evident. This torrent coming over the levee was a trickle, just moments ago. Now, it is a stream and may soon be a river. Here is Coli Duncan, our local news reporter to explain why this is a problem."

"Many parts of New Orleans are below sea level and miles of levees keep our rivers and lakes where they need to stay." Coli took a deep breath and continued, "Over the years extensive use of the waterways with more and larger ships has created more pressure on aging levees. Many local politicians and residents have petitioned state and federal governments for more funds and a comprehensive plan for updating existing levees, but as yet have not received the necessary funding." Roger gave Coli a chopping signal on the last sentence. She knew better than to go on.

Roger and Coli returned to the van. Now that they were out of immediate danger she remembered once again how tired she was. Her head still hurt. They drove for a block or two and then had to get out to remove the smaller branches and debris off the road. They detoured around the bigger trees, walls, and downed electrical wires on the roads. The trip back took three times as long as the trip out, but finally, they hauled themselves back to the hotel parking lot.

Roger fussed in the back of the van sending out more footage. Coli leaned against the back of her seat and closed her eyes. She was so tired and her head still hurt.

She was aroused by Roger. He had finished and they both needed to go into the hotel. Coli hoped to collapse in bed very soon. They trailed through the lobby. Three men in scruffy looking clothing were watching the news. Coli realized that it was her, centre front in storm torn New Orleans. She heard herself saying, " This is Coli Duncan at the Riverside Hotel, New Orleans, signing off.".

She felt so proud of herself. She saw the scene continuing. "Look out!" A hotel coffee maker came out of nowhere and crashed into Coli's head. She slumped onto the ground. Much bumpy camera shots and then Roger saying, "She's coming around now. Just a glancing blow. All in a day's work here at the biggest hurricane of the century in New Orleans."

Coli felt like she had been punched in the stomach. A bright red tide of embarrassment washed up her face. "Roger, how could you? It was a flying coffee machine that hit me?

"Don't worry, Ms. Sensitive. You're fine. You didn't need 911."

"Not that. You kept filming me and sent it out. You didn't tell me."

"Come on. The viewers love it. You saw their reaction." He pointed to the three guys still glued to the screen. "Look at their reaction. All sympathy. Poor brave you."

"It was great to start with but you should have stopped filming when I was hit."

"What? Avoid that great object lesson? In high winds, even some little thing as benign as a $10 coffee maker can be dangerous to an intrepid, non-observant cub reporter." Roger trailed off on a giggle.

"Do you do this to all your new partners?"

"Sure. Consider it a hazing ritual."

"Into what?—-the proud and ancient Order of Media Journalists?"

"Sure." Roger turned his back. "Be ready. Tomorrow, lobby, 6:30 am."

Coli struggled up the stairs to her room. Her head still hurt. Her pride had been mangled by Roger's human interest cameo of her collapse. Round and round all the scenes of destruction whirled and whirled in her mind. Excitement and shock pushed her as far as her room where she collapsed in bed. Her head still hurt and she was suddenly at the end of her strength. A shower was forgotten as sleep swallowed her.

CHAPTER 11

DON'T BLAME ME

Coli could barely contain her excitement. Roger had actually been able to get them on to a rescue helicopter. She and many others had thought that the city had survived the worst of the storm, but no one had seriously thought of how bad the flooding would be after the storm surge had passed. Everyone, except Reverend Weekes, had been in denial about the strength of the levees. When they were breached the city had begun to fill like a bowl.

Coli could not believe the scene spread out below her. Acres of water where it should not be. Roofs and treetops were showing above the murky waves and far too many people were waving desperately from rooftops. The helicopter was already full. The evacuees were packed in as tightly as possible. All of them sat or lay as quietly as they could, taking up as little room as possible. Coli noticed that everyone was looking down. They avoided looking at the reporters and all their equipment.

All of the evacuees needed some quality time with their hair stylist and a hot shower wouldn't go down badly either. The smells of too many people with too little sanitation permeated the hold. One guy was huddled beside a mom with two young kids. His carefully chosen bright-green and orange shirt was crumpled and dirty. His many dreadlocks were shiny and tangled. He just kept looking down, too dispirited to care.

The little boy beside him whimpered as he pushed into his mother's side. She sat with her legs out in front, clothed in a shapeless grey t-shirt and tattered jeans. Whether they were stylish or just ill-used was hard to tell at this point. She kept her head down too and watched her toddler, asleep against her other side.

Coli had tried to interview the evacuees at first but they all had the same story—disbelief at the rising water, a panicked scramble to the attic window, the long tedious wait, the relief at being picked up. They were surrounded by the crumpled debris of MRE's, rumoured to be life sustaining food. Now they were just waiting, with numb shock and disbelief, to start their real lives again.

Coli was starting to feel as enervated as the evacuees. She had been excited at first. She had taken some unbelievable shots. It would be great coverage to feed into the satellite. However, as the day progressed, she had become more and more overwhelmed. The sheer size of the disaster shocked her. The hopelessness of some of the rooftop groups distressed her and the slowness with which the rescue personnel could help people depressed her. This would probably be their last flight and there were still far too many people who would have to spend another night on their roofs. She only hoped that the water was at its peak now.

Wait a minute! Was that the church steeple in the Ninth Ward sticking up from the waves? A panicky thought escaped from the bottom of her mind where she had deliberately buried her fears about her mother. What was that huge shape coming into view?

It looked like a barge smashed against some houses. Crumpled roofs were protruding from the edges of the barge. A small tide line of debris washed up against it. Coli turned back and looked at the steeple. No! No! she thought. It couldn't be. Not her mama's place! No, please God. Mama didn't deserve this.

She heard Roger saying, "What's wrong with you?" He turned and saw her white face. "Don't faint on me now." She felt him push her head down and heard him muttering, "What a mess! Not now, you dizzy dame, not now."

A Message from Katrina

When she came to she was lying on the tarmac and most of the evacuees were gone from the helicopter. Roger seemed to be trying very hard not to start shouting. His loud voice ground through her headache. "I'll deal with her. I know you have enough to do without catering to reporters but I just can't stop now. We still haven't seen most of the flooded areas."

She couldn't hear the mumbled response from the pilot but she did hear Roger's voice. He seemed to be speaking through clenched teeth. "I don't care that your orders have changed! We were assured full cooperation! You'll be hearing from me tomorrow. Best American News' lawyers will have something to say about this," snarled Roger. His gaze swung around to Coli.

"Welcome back, Sleeping Beauty." He grabbed her under the armpits and hauled her to her feet. "Grab your stuff and hurry up," he barked. "Pull your weight around here."

Coli did the best she could but the trip back to the hotel seemed to be a slow motion horror show. The van had to be driven very carefully. Tree branches, and sometimes complete trees, littered the road. Debris from buildings had been piled up by the wind and high water. They had to double back and detour frequently to avoid the flooded low spots. At least they could drive here, as opposed to the completely flooded areas they had flown over today.

Finally, Roger pulled into the hotel parking lot and killed the motor in a shaded spot close to the building. He pointedly said nothing to Coli but did go around and open her door. She tumbled out of the van and staggered toward the back. She mumbled, "I'll help you with the editing, Roger".

Roger turned and stopped so fast that Coli collided with his chest. He hissed, "You've already done enough today. Anymore of your 'help' and our partnership is over. Go get some rest if you expect to tag along after me tomorrow." He turned on his heel and stomped to the back doors of the van.

Furiously, Coli turned towards the hotel. Her anger propelled her through the dim lobby. This time she didn't even try to tamp down her rage. Only the emergency lights were on and there was no smell of food emanating from the direction of the dining room. Of course, the elevator was not functioning. Electric power was a thing of the past and hopefully of the future.

Coli stomped up the stairs, each footstep releasing a bit more angry energy. She railed against herself. Stupid fool. She really had over-reacted. She couldn't handle the stress of being a reporter. Roger was right. She wasn't ready for the Big Time.

A Message from Katrina

Of course she shouldn't have let her personal fears for her mother interfere with her professional duties. Her mama had to have left town. She couldn't have stayed in the trailer. That barge couldn't have hit her mama's trailer. Too awful, and she had responded by fainting. There's a really tough media reporter for you.

Why should she expect Roger to have the extra strength to do more to support her? She realized that she was not being fair to Roger, but she couldn't do any better right now.

Orlando would have helped her more and not criticized her. Coli realized that in all the excitement and exhaustion of getting the job done she had not thought much about him. What kind of a self–centred moron was she? Her shoe suddenly caught in a hole in the cement step and she had to clutch the railing. Was there no end to these stairs?

Her longing for Orlando's support caught up with her again. Where was he? She had been trying hard not to worry about him but now his face kept surfacing in her mind. Yeah, when she needed him. Coli vaguely remembered him saying something about evacuating to Grand Falls. She really hoped he had.

She started berating herself for how she had handled their last few minutes together. Once she knew about the job she had run out on him with hardly a thought. Once again she despaired. What kind of idiot am I she wondered? With her mama, no, she couldn't go there, she thought as she started to feel light-headed and nauseous again.

She staggered up one more flight of stairs. Finally in her room, she dug into her suitcase and found one of her tins of sardines and a bottle of water. The junk food she and Roger had consumed in the van had not been a good substitute for real food. She hadn't realized that she was hungry but the tin was empty almost as soon as she took her first bite.

Coli crawled into bed and willed herself to sleep but she was much too agitated. Each time she closed her eyes she saw the barge crushing a building too much like her mama's trailer. She couldn't face that thought. She wouldn't acknowledge the worst until she could no longer avoid it. Maybe her mama had left in the bus as she had urged her to. At least Orlando had said he was going to Grand Falls. She belatedly wondered why, but at the same time was grateful that he had told her.

Then, her thoughts charged on to roots of trees across a road, then to the water lapping around the knees of people huddled on rooftops. When she deliberately tried to slow her thoughts down, she would visualize the corpses, drifting slowly in the currents of the water, their swollen bodies seeming to respond to music in a macabre, silent dance. She was scared.

She'd never get to sleep like this. She screamed silently. "Turn it off. Turn it off. Gotta sleep. Can't sleep. Gotta sleep. Can't sleep," became her mantra again. Then, without warning, she fell into a deep, black hole of exhaustion.

CHAPTER 12

FEAR ALWAYS TRIUMPHS

Coli staggered into the lobby. In spite of being exhausted, she hadn't slept very well. Her mind kept replaying her last conversation with her mother. She remembered how Charlene had refused to leave town, feeling that she could ride out the storm, as she had so many times before. The image of the barge and the crushed houses and trailers was burned into Coli's memory.

Her brain replayed that image again and again. She decided that she must shove that fear into the back of her mind until she could find out whether that was her mother's trailer and whether her mother was still there. Finally, she had fallen deep into a dark slumber. So, it was no surprise that she was a little wobbly this morning.

She wrinkled up her nose. What a welcome, but unexpected smell! Ah, freshly brewed coffee. She followed her nose into the restaurant and found the coffee urn with some sandwiches sitting beside it. The waitress took Coli's room number and told her that everyone was rationed to one cup of coffee and one sandwich.

Coli sensed a story and asked her why she was at work when thousands had fled. The waitress, Sandi, explained that she had survived the storm, but when the waters started rising, she figured she would do better at the hotel. She had been allowed to set up a cot in a storage room. The generators could handle the coffee urn, but she had started emptying out the fridges in case the power took a while to come on again because of all the damage.

While Coli was enjoying her hot coffee, Roger appeared. As usual, he ruined the moment. "Glad to hear you're up, Sleeping Beauty. Thanks to you, we're banned from the helicopters. Gimme that coffee and find us a boat." Coli quickly gulped down her coffee and handed him the empty cup. A new day, but not a new man she thought. Sandi took one look at him and decided that maybe it wasn't the right time to ask for his room number.

Coli navigated Roger and the van through the maze of streets and blockages. More people were out and about. Many were dressed in clothes they wouldn't have considered wearing three days ago. Most had probably used up the supplies they had bought before the storm. Any open stores could be doing quite well if anyone had any money left. Very few police or emergency responders seemed to be on the streets yet. Coli stared, looking carefully at the faces of those on the streets. She had to find someone she knew. Hopefully someone she knew with a boat.

Coli was lucky. She led them to the east side of the city where the flooding had been the deepest. Near the foot of the St. Claude Street Bridge she found Jackson Poirier, a tough kid she remembered from school. When he saw the color of their money he was willing to stop ferrying the roof clingers to the bridge and take on a paying tour for the day. Coli tried to ignore her disquiet at jumping the queue of evacuees. She quieted her conscience with thoughts of her job. She had a mission. Reporting the situation would bring more help than just a boat!

She and Roger filled their cameras with images of the drowned streets. They filmed several different groups of foragers or looters, depending on your point of view. The men didn't seem to be concerned that their faces might appear on the evening news. Jackson piloted Coli and Roger around flaming houses, shops and warehouses, most of which were in the process of burning to the waterline. Some firefighters were out, but there were far too few men and machines to handle all the fires that were burning.

A Message from Katrina

Debris swirled and floated on the water. Oily patches and nasty smelling eddies were starting to proliferate. Corpses of people and animals were beginning to bloat and awful smells were getting stronger. Coli ached to be able to do something to bring the city back to its normal life.

Roger kept filming with a grim kind of excitement. Towards the end of their day, Jackson piloted their boat around the corner of a tree-lined street, aptly named Willow Avenue. A long building spread out behind a low and mostly submerged hedge. The sign above the door had water lapping below its words, Resthaven, Seniors' Home. It seemed eerily quiet. Roger called out to Jackson, "Go over there. I want to try to see in the tops of the windows." Some were covered by drapes, but some were open.

To her horror, Coli found herself looking at a body floating face down in water above the bed in the room. The long white hair was spread out like a halo around the back of the head. A white nightgown floated calmly around the thin body and arms. Before she could quite take in the full meaning of the scene, the boat had carried her to another window. Inside she saw the tops of metal poles with IV lines swirling around another corpse of an old man, whose open eyes seemed to be staring straight at her with reproach. She felt the remains of her breakfast rising up and quickly stuck her face over the edge of the boat, adding to the unsavoury nature of the water swirling around them.

When she looked up, Roger too, was staring at her with reproach. "How could anyone leave them?" she whispered in horror.

"Fear always triumphs," Roger replied coldly. "The best we can do is make them pay. I've got the name of the facility. I'll have the office research who owns it. There could be quite a story here. Let's head back now and get these shots out to the evening news."

CHAPTER 13

REFUGE OR JAIL?

As Jackson piloted his boat through water which had risen since yesterday, Coli could see the Convention Center growing larger. The sun still shone in a clear blue sky. The day was going to be every bit as hot and humid as all the others since the hurricane had passed through. The smells on the water and in the city continued to multiply and mix in a way that Coli had never experienced before and never wanted to again. They had gone past groups of people, who seemed strangely subdued. They seemed to be in shock or stoically waiting to be rescued, so that they could restart their normal lives. Fewer police seemed to be on search and rescue. More police seemed to be out trying to deal with looting and arson. There was also a military presence in the city, giving out water and MREs. Meals Ready to Eat seemed to be an optimistic description but hunger did blunt the taste buds.

Coli and Roger, guided by Jackson, skirted around groups, mostly men with raised voices and sometimes raised fists. They detoured around anything burning, always afraid that a gas main could suddenly rupture. Finally, they arrived near the crowds outside the Convention Center. Jackson Poirier eased the boat behind some large dumpsters and hunkered down to watch it while Coli and Roger went off to do some interviews.

There were some family groups outside the doors. The older and sick-looking adults were huddled or slumped in lawn chairs or folding chairs. They were staring into space or resting with closed eyes. Children were huddled near them. Some people had suitcases or bags nearby. Others were huddled on tarps on the lawn or sidewalks. Garbage was everywhere. The bins were full. Empty water and pop bottles were scattered all around. Plastic bags and other litter carpeted the area between clusters of people. Most people just sat waiting for their lives to begin again. They were still recovering from the shock of what had happened.

"Come on. It's bound to be worse inside," said Roger. He and Coli pushed open the doors and were almost knocked backwards by the fetid air that hit them like a fist.

"Ugh," said Coli, starting to cough.

"Come on," said Roger. "I've smelled worse. After a few minutes your nose goes on strike and it's not so bad."

Coli tried to ignore the smell and keep her stomach contents where they should be. She introduced herself as a reporter for Best American News and started her interviews. Most people were waiting for food; the MREs had yet to arrive inside. People were also waiting for buses. The city was still under evacuation orders and anyone left at this point, had no choice. They had to leave when the buses arrived. They were surprised that nothing had arrived yet but had no better options than to wait. Coli talked to a young family whose home was underwater, but even so, they were thankful and optimistic because they had been rescued and no one had been hurt. Coli saw a young woman putting rollers into an older woman's hair. She hustled over.

"Hi, I'm Coli Duncan from Best American News," she said. "Why are you doing hair?" The girl looked up at her.

"Hi, I'm Sherri. I like doing hair. I figured it might be sort of boring waiting in here so I brought my hair stuff." She snapped her gum with every second word. Coli didn't want to think about how long she might have been chewing that particular wad.

"I brought my scissors too so it looks like I got lots of clients." She waved her hands around the scene of thousands of people all looking in need of a bit of hair care.

Coli turned her camera and commented into it, "In spite of all the difficulties inherent in the events of the last five days, people here are doing whatever they can to make things better for themselves and others." She went through the crowd, choosing to interview those who seemed to be coping and helping others. She was feeling very pleased with herself.

From time to time she caught glimpses of Roger. He seemed to be drawn to the raised voices, raised fists, and groups tense with incipient violence. She caught him once or twice panning the piles of debris and worse at the edges of the Centre. She saw an area that seemed to have several body bags grouped together. Roger was talking to an attendant nearby. Then he started to head into the crowd again and she lost sight of him. She needed to find some fresh interviews. There was a woman with six young children around her. Coli wondered what her story was. She started to move towards the little group.

Roger came up behind her and grabbed her arm. "Quick, outside! Shots fired!" They ran toward the nearest exit. Once outside they slid along the wall. Looking around the corner, Roger started his camera. Coli could see a helicopter trying to land as she heard the muted sounds of gunfire. She could see the National Guard inside lowering boxes of water bottles and what she took to be MREs to the crowd below who had suddenly flattened themselves out on the sidewalk to avoid the gunfire.

Suddenly the helicopter rose up and headed away. The shots stopped soon after. The people on the ground looked around cautiously and then started to scramble to the nearest water bottles. Roger grabbed Coli again. "Let's get out of here. This will be great on the evening news! Military bringing supplies fired on! Only in America." He almost crowed with excitement.

"You don't know that they were firing on the helicopter," puffed Coli as she ran after him.

"Of course they were, Miss Pollyanna," returned Roger as he carefully lifted the camera into the boat. Jackson had the boat quietly put-putting away almost before Coli had her last leg in.

"You always think the worst, Roger. I talked to some perfectly normal people inside who were doing the best that they could, without violence."

"Pretty boring," sneered Roger. "Nobody turns on the news to see Mrs. Nice slumped comatose in a lawn chair. You've got to look for the excitement, something that will create excitement or fear in the viewers. Make them glad they're not here, even if they're in a tenement in Chicago."

Coli feared he was right but she didn't have to like it.

Finally, Coli and Roger climbed out of the van near their hotel. Roger put out his hand to take Coli's camera and start the editing process in the back of the van. Coli held back and said, "I want to help in the editing. I've got some really good interviews of people making the best of things. I really admire their courage."

"You still don't get it." Roger said wearily. "People don't want to see Pollyanna smiling in the face of adversity."

"Why are you so sure they want to see the mess and the random violence?" retorted Coli.

"Don't be stupider than necessary," snarled Roger. "Every bit of disorder and villainy titillates their sense of security sitting in their armchairs in front of the TV screen." Roger put out his hand again for Coli's camera. She backed up, away from him.

"What are you afraid of, Roger? Do you think that after five days on the job I'm a threat to your position? Do you think that I'm going to go into that van, elbow you aside and do a better job?" asked Coli.

Roger raised his fist. Then, he realized what he had started to do. He turned bright red in the face. He grabbed Coli's camera out of her hands, walked to the door of the van, and yanked it open. He slammed the door and left Coli's ears ringing with his controlled violence.

The next six days of working with Roger didn't get any better. She focused on the stoicism and bravery of people; and Roger looked for the extreme and terrible. Too much of the city was still flooded. The levees were built up again but the pumps couldn't be repaired because the replacement parts had not been manufactured for years. Replacement parts had to be specially machined, delaying the removal of floodwaters.

In spite of these maddening delays with the levees, human help was starting to make a difference. The presence of the police and volunteer aid workers started to be felt. The military converged in large numbers with food and water. Bus transportation finally arrived at the Convention Center and the Super Dome, and extra flights arrived for the remaining evacuees. Roger and Coli found more than enough exciting footage. They watched their own coverage on the evening news and even had a little time to watch their competitors.

Coli was appalled when they saw a sniper shooting at helicopters brought in to evacuate the sickest patients from a hospital. Roger was envious that they had missed it. They saw the local politicians were pleading for more help. They heard the state politicians trying to keep local control of the situation and the federal agencies blaming each other for the lack of a swift response.

By the ninth day after the arrival of Hurricane Katrina, the pumps were finally working and most of the city's population had been evacuated. The show was over, for now. Coli and Roger received their stand down call.

CHAPTER 14

GOOD-BYE TO NEW ORLEANS

Coli struggled with the key. Her apartment door squealed open and she staggered into the hall, dropped her grip and looked toward her meagre living room and kitchen space . She was glad to collapse on the couch for a minute. Funny, she didn't feel her usual sense of relief and welcome in being home. Maybe she was in shock from the excitement of the last few days. Good thing that Roger had become friendlier with the impending dissolution of their partnership. He had helped her grab her stuff and even drove her back to her apartment. He had been willing to take her north in the van tomorrow.

Beneath the shock and relief, Coli felt lucky. Her apartment building was still standing. A treetop had slammed up against the far end of the building, but there was no damage near her apartment. The French Quarter was on high ground, so it had escaped the flooding. She tried to flick on a light. Nothing happened. She tried another switch. Still no light. Her luck had ended. The power was out and probably would be for a few more days. She tried the water in the sink. Only a gurgle and a cough. No water either. It was a good thing that Coli had brought her last tin of sardines and two water bottles from the hotel. If the toilet held a tank full of water she would be all right for the night.

She staggered over to the window, banging her knee on the coffee table in the process. She shoved up the old window and pushed open the heavy shutters. Those old shutters had saved her apartment from the wind. She looked around her rooms, bathed in the glow of the evening sunlight. She had loved this apartment. It represented her freedom from the poverty of her childhood and her drunken, irritable mother. She remembered her joy here with Orlando.

She couldn't recover any of those feelings. Her fear for her mother was tightly wrapped and hidden from sight. She would deal with it later. Her joy in Orlando's company had also been tucked away until she had time to deal with it. He had said he was going to Grand Falls. She would try to find him. She felt both excited and fearful. She had left without a backward glance after all, but then she had needed to block him from her thoughts, several times a day in fact. Maybe she had been as much in shock as anyone she had interviewed. The feelings she had held at bay were starting to creep out at her but she really didn't want to deal with any feelings right now. She looked around her wonderful apartment, acquired with such triumph. It was now only a pleasant space, empty of the people she loved and curiously empty of any future for her.

Well, thought Coli as she waited for Roger to pick her up next morning at her apartment, her big break had not gone exactly as she had always dreamed it would. She had worked with a famous on-camera reporter, a living icon in the news world. He had been hardworking, meticulous, and grudgingly taught her as little as he needed her to know.

It hadn't been a warm, fuzzy experience. He had seemed openly contemptuous of her most of the time. She could only remember one or two compliments that seemed to fall from unwilling lips. Talk about two solitudes! Two solitudes? Where had that come from? Coli tried to think. Yes, she almost had it—McClellan, no McInnis, no, maybe McClelland. That was right, a Canadian novel by a guy called McClelland. *Two Solitudes*.

She had read it when she took that Canadian lit course because it was the only one that fit into her waitressing hours. What was it about? Two Solitudes were the French and the English in Canada. They didn't understand each other's culture. She couldn't remember much more about it. She could handle beginnings and crises: she just couldn't seem to pay attention to the middle stuff.

Had the English and French ever learned to understand each other's cultures? She had no idea what had finally happened in the book. Canadian history didn't help much either. The bit the lit prof had mentioned was so boring that Coli had barely listened.

She and Roger were like that, two solitudes. They had worked closely for the past ten days but any hero-worshipping that she had done in the past was well and truly shattered.

He sure looked like he could support you with his infinite knowledge and wisdom on TV but he certainly didn't want to share very much of that with her. He had efficiently done the job with her but she didn't really know anything about him. Did he have any family? He'd never mentioned any. Mind you, she hadn't exactly been loquacious about her mother. Even after her panic attack she didn't mention anything but the bare essentials. She hadn't even considered mentioning Orlando to him. Maybe Roger had built a prickly hedge around his private life, but it wasn't as if she had been overly friendly either. They had both just wanted to get the job done, while, of course, showering themselves with glory.

She heard her intercom buzz and decided that she'd make an effort to be more human or at least friendly on the trip to Grand Falls.

CHAPTER 15

INTERREGNUM

Coli dragged her sore and exhausted body out of Roger's van. Talk about ten days of stress! Maybe she had even lost some weight. She looked around blearily and saw Roger's face with its ready sneer. "Exactly why do you want me to drop you here? This place looks like it was falling apart before Katrina. Then, the die-hards taped it together here and there for awhile. But look at it now, complete chaos."

Coli noticed that every empty lot and every large parking lot was filled with tents, government issued travel trailers and building debris. The campgrounds by the river looked completely overwhelmed too. There was a huge tent with a Red Cross symbol above it, probably an outdoor kitchen or food depot. Port-a-potties were deposited like tiny tool sheds across the townscape. She looked at Roger wearily and tried to sound confident as she said, "This is a town and a community rebuilding. It's messy. Not everybody can spend all their time and energies titillating the viewing public, like you, Roger. Not everybody can spend their time crafting sound bytes from the latest crisis. Most people have to live with the results."

"Brave words," he bit out. "We'll see how you feel after a week here in Nowheresville. Watch for the next crisis. Coli Duncan, intrepid cub reporter, will snap it up. See you in the news, kid!" With that updated Casa Blanca exit line, he revved the engine and headed north to whatever he called family.

Coli sighed. She had tried friendly, but she just couldn't remain friendly with Roger's cynicism and constant criticism. She was exhausted to the bone. She needed someone who appreciated her. She needed someone who loved her. She let that sealed off corner of her mind open again. She needed Orlando.

How to find him? Coli looked up the main street; already regretting her impetuous flight. As if she had taken any care with his feelings or their relationship the last time she had seen him. How could she have run out on him with only seconds of agonizing? Right! The career comes first. She hadn't known then how draining she would find the pain and exhaustion of too much catastrophe, too much shock. She had seen too many people who could not comprehend what had happened to them. She feared that at any minute she might just sit down and never move again. She didn't feel ready to do anything constructive about living her life again. She had only one thought-find Orlando.

She picked a direction at random and started to walk. There were knots of people on the street as well as adults and children peering out of tents and travel trailers. Most people had the same shocked and weary look in their eyes. They seemed to be asking, "What next?" If Coli could figure that out herself, she'd be happy to share it. She heard some music and turned up a side street towards it. She strained to catch the words.

> "Our future can be bright
> If we treat our planet right.
> And we can carry on, can carry on
> Yes, we can!"

Well, that at least seemed a thin thread of hope. But, the next verse fitted right in with the dirge-like tune,

> "Hurricanes roared in to break them,
> Coastal cities, rich and proud.
> Shattered bits among the high tides,
> Was all the future, storms allowed."

The words tripped a vague memory, but she couldn't bring it forward into her conscious mind. She stopped to ask one of the young guys in the back of the group.

"What's the song? I think I've heard it before."

He turned and looked at her in amazement. Coli noticed his messy hair, dark eyebrows and intense eyes. "Everybody's singing it. It's called 'The New Earth Song'. Some of us think it ought to be called 'Gaia's Revenge'," he muttered as he deliberately looked away.

'Gaia's Revenge'? Coli turned that over in her mind. She knew that name Gaia. It was coming back to her now. She remembered one of the speakers at the Emerging Weather Trends Conference. He had proposed the name Gaia to refer to all the interconnected systems that support the balance of planet Earth. One of the speakers had even imbued the concept with a consciousness for survival. Just a minute. She had just caught hold of another memory. Rev. Weekes' choir had been singing that same song when she did the interview. Then it had seemed far-fetched; now, it just seemed like a realistic commentary. Maybe the chorus was even a little too optimistic. She came out of her introspection. Something had caught her eye.

Wait. What was that sign? She moved her head and eyes back to the painted sign. It was big and bright but nobody could accuse it of being professional looking. It was above a door that was solid but had seen better days. BIG EASY MOVES. Big easy moves? She puzzled it out —a restaurant? No. A new gym in town. No. Not now. Suddenly she got it and started to laugh. It had to be a club, a new nightclub. She knew someone with a mind like that, someone whom she really wanted to see. She started heading up the street towards the sign.

The place had that somewhat deserted and flat look of a club in daylight. It was early in the afternoon, too early for any action, but the staff might be there. They might know something about a band or a musician. She pushed through the unlocked door and struggled with all her gear into a large room. The dimly lit space had the usual scuffed tables, leatherette covered chairs, a large bar and a small stage at one end. The walls were mud coloured and decorated with beer and whiskey posters. She heard the door at the other end open and caught a whiff of what could be food being prepared. But what stopped her in her tracks was the shape of the person emerging from the doorway.

"Orlando!" she called out. She started to rush towards him but then checked herself. She had forfeited any right to think that he might welcome her. She watched the surprise on his face change to welcome. He made a step towards her, and then he also checked himself. His smile of welcome became uncertain.

Coli had rehearsed this meeting more than once, repeatedly in fact. Asleep and in daydreams that sealed off part of her mind kept opening up. The details and the ending kept slipping, sliding, and morphing into panic-producing scenarios.　Stick to the plan she told herself. Start out how you want to go on.　Go for what you want, not what you deserve, or what you fear will happen.

"In spite of everything that's been happening, I've missed you."　She tried to say it with determination and passion but it came out breathless and quavering. Fear pulsed through her. Pull yourself together she thought.

Orlando's wariness started to creep in the direction of welcome again.　He seemed to be considering what to say before he opened his mouth.　In fact, he often paused to think before talking, a characteristic that Coli really liked, in principle.　Right now, his reticence was beginning to worry her.　He seemed to make his decision.　He started to walk towards her and said, "I haven't missed you at all." She felt her whole inner self crumble.　She had thrown her future with Orlando away for a few hours of panic, excitement and exhaustion.　Oh, and fame and money. They had been distracting.

"In fact", he continued with his slow smile, "I watched you whenever I could.　'This is Coli Duncan, Best American News reporter from hurricane-ravaged New Orleans.　The devastation is overwhelming but the courage of ordinary people to just keep going has been extraordinary.' I like your point of view. You were trying to make ordinary people noble and strong when other reporters seemed to be concentrating on all the violence, lies, and incredible disorganization.

"I needed to see you in the flesh, but that didn't seem to be a possibility, so I made do."

"You can see me in the flesh now." Coli tried her best to be flirtatious.

"Not quite enough flesh," replied Orlando, with even more of a smile in his voice.

"We could solve that problem pretty quick."

"I don't have much of a place yet, a couple of rooms over the club. Come on." He finally came close enough to give her the hug and the kiss she had been hoping for. He grabbed her and started for the stairs.

The room wasn't much, but it did have a mattress on the floor - not exactly a Louisiana Plantation bed. It also contained a chair and several boxes that seemed to be standing in for bedroom furniture. "I couldn't bring much when I left and supplies have been limited just lately," Orlando said with a grin.

He turned to her and the chaos in the room faded out for both of them.

Much later, they were snuggled together in a restful sleep. Coli awoke and looked at Orlando. She finally took the time to enjoy her pleasure at the sight of him. She loved his smooth, brown skin; his short curly hair; his fine, long musician's fingers, and compact, strong body. Love made her see him anew as too valuable to walk away from.

He opened his eyes and smiled at her. He saw her looking at him with love in her eyes. He said, "I knew you had to do it, but I didn't need to be happy about it."

"Why didn't you talk me out of it?" she teased.

He laughed, "Talk you out of it? You were moving like a freight train. I tried to stop you at the door, but you barely had time to say 'good-bye'."

"All right. I admit it. It was my big chance. It was exciting, frustrating and overwhelming."

"You looked pretty professional. You really have become a household name. But there was one time when you didn't look too good. What happened?"

"When?" queried Coli, as anxiety coiled inside her stomach.

"You seemed to be in a helicopter. It was three or four days after the first storm surge. The levees had broken and the lower parishes had started to fill up. You were giving an aerial view of the worst flooding. I caught a glimpse of that huge barge that had come loose and crashed into a couple of houses. Then, suddenly, you weren't on the camera anymore. It was Roger Silverfox who was going on about all the flooded houses and people waiting to be rescued on the roofs."

Coli started to shiver and clenched her teeth, hoping it would stave off the panic attack that seemed to be hovering very near. "I think it landed on my mother's trailer. I'm not sure whether she was still there. We had a fight just before the hurricane arrived. I told her to leave and she refused. I haven't heard from her since. I need to see someone tomorrow and register to get news about her. I've, I've been trying not to think about it," she stuttered. "But I've got to face it. I'm as bad as all those people I saw in shock. Just sitting there, waiting for someone else to jump start their lives again." She trailed away into silence.

Orlando looked at her in amazement. "I didn't realize that you didn't know," he said slowly, " or I would've told you right away. Your mama is here in town."

"Here, in town !" Coli echoed in amazement. "Did you talk to her?"

"She wouldn't talk to me, Coli."

"Then, are you sure it's her?"

"If it's not her, then her twin is working at *Cost Effective Cuts.*"

Coli felt a thunder in her ears. She shouted, "My mother is here, alive and well in Grand Falls? I thought she was dead! That big barge was lying on top of where her trailer used to be. That's when I turned white and fainted, off camera. Roger took over in a hurry. Of all the irresponsible things she's done, this takes the cake."

She could feel a huge wave of rage building inside her. Oh no, she thought, this has happened before. She both hated and feared her sudden overwhelming rages. Even so, she was caught in its power and an image of herself on a surfboard hurtling on the edge of the wave thrust into her mind. She was not riding the wave in control. She was holding on for dear life and very close to losing it completely. She could hear someone close to her swearing.

"How could she? How could she? " punctuated her rage. "How could she argue with me, lie to me, and then leave and not tell me?" shouted Coli. She noticed that she was methodically slamming one fist into the open palm of her other hand. She also noticed that Orlando had backed up to the edge of the bed and was looking at her cautiously. Well, I guess this is better than throwing glasses or chairs, Coli thought as she tried hard to slow down and keep her hands still.

Orlando mentioned reluctantly, "You have been a little hard to contact lately."

Coli turned her gaze to him. She noticed that her fist had uncurled and that her hands were almost still. "I don't have a cell phone or I would have called you first.

By the time I realized that a cell phone would be useful, there was no way to get one." She glared at Orlando. "Don't you take her part against me," she moaned. Then she continued more calmly, "Even when it is perfectly justified."

"You are one very scary woman when you're mad," replied Orlando. He ventured closer to Coli and she couldn't stop herself from leaning into his arms. She let herself go for a few hysterical sobs and then quieted down to the heart-felt relief of a good cry.

If Orlando had the courage to hold her after a meltdown like that, there was hope for their future yet, thought Coli with relief.

"When you've cooled down. You know, in a year or two." He looked cautiously at Coli. His slow smile moved tentatively across her face. "You need to go over or call her," he finished, trying hard to gauge her mood. He hugged her again. "Mama, used to tell me that fear and anger were cell mates. When one was let loose, the other came too."

Maybe Orlando's mama was right. With his second embrace, Coli could feel herself returning to her more normal, rational self. She prided herself on her ability to feel the heat and move on.

CHAPTER 16

STAND DOWN

Charlene heard the door of *Cost Effective Cuts* open and close as she was bent over, organizing her workstation one more time. Good, she thought, it's been a real slow morning. More like a real slow week since the hurricane. I guess, people got more to worry about than their hair but I really need some income. I'm not like Coli, making money from a disaster. She turned just as her potential customer spoke up.

"My life-long barber died."

"Yeah, it happens." Charlene looked up to see a small muscular man, only a few inches taller than she was. His well-seasoned cowboy hat added a few inches more and the high heeled boots a few more. A real bantam rooster of a man. "Y'all got any hair under there that needs cutting? We do that here y' know, cut hair, doesn't matter

166

your sex or who you love, we cut hair. Then, you fork over a lot of money."

Ray looked a little closer. He liked a sparky woman. He'd missed that in the years since his wife had died. The woman in the hair stylist apron was short, trim and pretty. Past her first flush of youth but that probably meant that she knew a thing or two. Dark, fine, curly hair and lots of it. From her French grandma or her black grandpa? He didn't know and didn't care. Maybe a woman cutting his hair opened up some new possibilities.

"If you still want your hair cut, even styled, my station's over here." She turned on her heel and marched past a woman with foil twisted tufts decorating her head at Grace's station. She was pleased now that her schedule had been light today. You never know.

Coli looked up at the sign, *Cost Effective Cuts*. It looked as if someone had washed it since the last time she had seen it. She gave a sigh as she opened the door. It had to be done. The smells were familiar, but thankfully the decades old photos of hot hairdos were no longer on the walls. Her mother had actually replaced them with a few modern shots. Coli could see a hairdresser snipping ends from hair of a very improbable colour. Just then, the hairdresser looked up and Coli was eye to eye with her mother.

There were no sighs of delight or hugs and kisses. "I figured you'd turn up soon, now that storm's over," muttered her mother.

"It's good to see you too, Mama," contributed Coli between clenched teeth. "Last time I talked to you, you weren't going to evacuate."

"So, now you're mad at me because I took your advice. I can't make you happy no matter what I do. Anyway, I already phoned Grace about the job. You always seemed so busy with your job that I thought you wouldn't miss me, so why wait? You got a place to stay? You can't stay with me. The apartment out back is about the size of a closet."

"Don't worry. I just came by to see that you're all right. I'm staying with Orlando," replied Coli.

Now it was Charlene's turn to be annoyed. "Just let that colour set for a few minutes. I'll be back in a moment," she said to her customer in a falsely pleasant voice and headed for the back room. Coli stormed after her.

Coli watched her mother search for cigarettes in her purse. The ritual of lighting up and taking the first drag seemed to calm her mother a bit. Coli was trying to calm her own feelings as she watched her mother pull a beer out of the fridge. Charlene turned the cap with practiced ease and took her first swallow with an air of desperation. "Grace knows the value of a lunch time beer," she commented. "For a reporter, you don't seem to notice much, Collette. That Orlando's just not good enough for you. You can do better. That Roger Silverfox, now he's someone you should be working on."

Coli tried to be reasonable and confident. She said, "We love each other. Orlando's started up a club here in town. At least he plans to stick around," she couldn't stop herself from adding,

Her mother looked stricken. "You always did know how to strike a low blow. You'd better leave now," she hissed.

Coli backed up with a feeling of defeat. She watched her mother looking determinedly out the window while smoke curled around her head. What is it about my mama and me she thought? Why didn't I just tell her how I feel? That I'm glad she made it through the storm and came here, but furious that I worried and grieved for her death.

Coli reminded herself that she was an adult now and a serious talk with her mother was long overdue. As it seemed like her mother was pointedly not talking to her, she had very little to lose. While she was trying to think of a way to start, her mother gave a long sigh, raised her shoulders, and looked at Coli.

"You can thank or blame Edna for what I'm going to say. She told me that I had to have a serious talk with you, just before she died." Charlene faltered. The silence of many years choked them both.

Just when Coli felt she had to say something to keep the connection going, Charlene looked at her with pleading in her eyes. "I was really young when I met Ed, just sixteen when we married. You know that I left home the year before, after Papa died and Mama went to visit with her Aunt Denise.

"I was lucky enough to meet Edna. I was about the same age as her girls. She saw that I was afraid and offered me a job cleaning up for my room and board. Then, she taught me how to cut hair and talk good to the clients. Just like you, I wouldn't listen when she told me that I could do better than Ed."

"You've never liked to talk about family to me."

Charlene looked surprised. "I already explained that there weren't nothing to tell. Mama and Papa loved me. Nobody hurt me. Mama did her best but Papa liked to drink as well as to go shrimping. We were dirt poor and I figured I could do better anywhere else. That shows how stupid I was." Charlene laughed hollowly remembering her dreams.

A Message from Katrina

She looked up at Coli. "Then there was Ed, exactly the dream I was looking for. We had so much fun, eating out, dancing, never a dull moment. Then he was gone again."

Charlene looked a question at Coli. "How much do you remember?" Before Coli could answer she went on. "He was a bus driver. He did the long haul up to the Great Lakes and back again. Gone two weeks and back for a few days. I thought the good times would last forever. Then I got pregnant with you." She stopped and gazed into the past.

Coli's stomach tightened with fear. She shoved away some vague but bad memories.

Charlene sighed again. "I already said I was young and stupid. Since then I've had lots of time to blame myself. So, yeah, at first I blamed you when I was big as a boat and couldn't go dancing. I blamed you some more when Ed got tired of a crying baby and a whining wife. I was jealous of every hug and bounce on the knee that he gave you. Looking back, I don't blame him as much as I did then, for taking the easy street.

"His trips kept taking longer and longer. He stayed with us less and less and then finally, he just didn't come back. You cried and cried for him and I blamed you some more. I found the same peace Papa was looking for in his bottle. It helped for a bit and still does," she finished, looking defiantly at Coli.

Coli stared back at her. She remembered her mama's words, "For a reporter, you don't notice much," and her comeback, "I'm focused—-just not on that." Now she realized that, for many years, she and her mama had very definitely avoided talking about her father and why he left. She had always felt guilty about something. Her mama had blamed her for the drinking more than once.

It helped to know why, but it didn't take away the pain. She supposed she should feel sad for that young girl. At least her mama and Edna had looked after her when she was a teenager. As unhappy as she had been, Coli had never considered running away.

Charlene and Coli just sat at the kitchen table, neither having any remedy for the past. Finally, Charlene said, "Her hair colour ain't never gonna be changed if I don't get out there now." Charlene pasted a smile on her face and went back to her customer.

Coli continued to sit. She couldn't do much more than breathe. Shock, that was it. She was in shock. Hurricane's could do it or strong feelings. She stumbled out the back door and walked past the minimal gardens, flattened by the high winds and days of rain. She looked up the street blindly. Well, I guess I should be used to it, she thought sourly. At least, I've got some time to sort it out with her. But not today.

Outside on the street most of the broken tree branches had been removed from the road and sidewalks, but some of the small ones were still littering the grass and the bedraggled flowerbeds. Even so far from New Orleans, the storm winds had created some damage.

Now, where would George set up shop? If she could find him, he might be happy to see her and hear about the details that didn't make it on air. She couldn't believe he'd be happy sitting in an RV in the park for long. She'd try the failed mall and then find the Red Cross centre. Somebody there would probably know of him.

As she came closer to the mall, she started to see more tents, trailers, and RV's on the side of the road and in all the parking lots. Finally she could see the mall lot, filled with people, tents, tarps, port-a-potties and noise. The Red Cross flag was flying from the Timothy Weekes auditorium, and a line up of resigned looking people was snaking out of its front door. One of the small shop fronts displayed the sign, ***Grand Falls News and Views***, **Your Local Station**. *We supply all your advertising needs.* Keep hoping, George, Coli thought to herself.

She pushed the door open and saw George's shaggy form hunched over his computer. "Well, Coli," he said, rising and giving her a bear hug. This is the way my mama should have greeted me thought Coli. "Good work on the storm. I guess you learned a lot from Roger 'cause you sure looked professional out there. Well, except for the coffee maker episode, but that was just bad luck." George regretted his last statement when he saw Coli's blush of embarrassment. He tried to recover. "I liked your human interest interviews too."

What else could she say except, "Thanks George."

"It was an eye-opener to see my childhood idol at work." I really got to see his clay feet too, she could have added, but figured it wouldn't help her in the long run. "I could do a few more for you."

"A few more what?" returned George with a puzzled frown.

"You know, human interest interviews, evacuees' experiences and their future plans. What next? That kind of thing. Plus some self-help information. If I talked to somebody at the Red Cross Centre, maybe we could help shorten that line outside. I saw that they had some TVs set up outside under the porch roof. You could add an electronic message board with some advertising, in case people are looking for businesses here in town. In fact, Orlando could advertise his club."

"Well, maybe Coli, but I'm not turning a profit yet so I couldn't offer you much as wages."

A Message from Katrina

"I've got my storm coverage money coming, so I could get by on not much for a while. When we're famous and pulling in the money, I'll expect a lot more though." Coli sighed. As if.

Next morning Coli was up early. She left Orlando sleeping after his late night in the pub. She spent some time placing her camera carefully in her new-to-her bike's basket and hefted her back pack of tapes and notebooks. She was glad that Grand Falls was small. Bus travel around town was not yet an option. She set off into the sun splashed morning.

Coli slipped into the EMPLOYEES ONLY door of the Red Cross Station. She found herself in the break room. Two young women looked up.

"Hi, I'm Coli Duncan from the local cable station. I'd like to interview you and find out how to help the evacuees and shorten your line-up outside."

"Now you're talking," said the dark-skinned girl in the chair. Her halo of curly black hair gave the height and substance that her short, slight frame certainly didn't offer. "Hi, I'm Doris. I'm at the desk out front most of the time. I reassure people that I can help them, given enough time and information."

"And what do people mostly need?"

"It was food at first, but now we have the food depot operating out of the tent at the back of the mall. We also have a kitchen for Red Cross helpers and those who would rather pay for rations than cook them."

"So what is it now?"

"Money. Lots of people have run out. At first, FEMA was giving out debit cards with $2000 attached but that didn't work because it soon got snarled up about who had been given what and who hadn't. That's where Martha here comes in"

Coli looked up at a very tall African-American woman. She was beautiful on a very large scale.

"She's one of those computer geeks that checks out everybody's information.   She keeps track of where everybody is and who was given what."

"Yes, we actually found Shaylene's baby yesterday. He had been evacuated to a hospital in Texas. In all the confusion and looking after her other kids, she had lost contact. She was going out of her mind with worry," added Martha in a warm voice. Her hand hit the side of her coffee cup. "Oops! Got it," she said as she grabbed the falling cup.

The door opened behind Coli. Doris jumped up and hugged the guy who came in. He looked like Doris's twin, same small body and big hair. He probably wasn't though, given his reaction to the embrace.

"Here's Kincaid, my boyfriend," said Doris.

"So, do you work for the Red Cross too?" asked Coli.

"No, I'm the accountant and equipment manager on Jubal Weekes' farm," replied Kincaid. This jiggled a memory in Coli's mind.

"I think we met a few weeks ago when Rev. Weekes brought his congregation out to see the town."

"Yeah, lots of them are here now. Not exactly the way we thought they'd arrive, but still, they're here. We'd hoped to have the condos completed first, but the storm has pushed everything back." Kincaid gave Doris another hug. "See you guys tonight over at Big Easy Moves. Nice meeting you, Coli." With that he was gone, in a swirl of flash and energy.

As he went out the door, a solidly built woman came in. Her black hair was swirled with gray and her skin glowed with health. "This is Jeanne. She's the top cook in the Red Cross kitchen by day and the pub by night. You know, Big Easy Moves. Her son Orlando runs it and plays there."

When Jeanne turned enough to see Coli, she gave a big smile and then hugged Coli hard. "I heard a lot about you, girl, and none of it bad. Now it's my turn to meet our rising media star."

Coli stepped out of the embrace, wondering how some mothers were so good at getting this whole relationship thing. Her worries about her welcome from Orlando's mother just drifted away. She smiled back and then started her interview about exactly what Jeanne's duties were, and how her catering business had been changed by Hurricane Katrina.

Then, Coli moved out to the line-up and continued interviewing. A mother, father and two young children needed some cash to head north to Chicago where family and a potential job waited. They said they wouldn't be back to New Orleans because their rented trailer had been under water for a week and they really didn't want to see what their meager possessions looked like.

A middle-aged teacher from Waveland wanted to set up classes here for a month or two. When the families left, she planned to head back to rebuild her house on the beach and help rebuild her town. No storm was going to tell her where to live.

Two teenagers had just returned from the remains of their grandmother's house in Mobile. There wasn't anything to go back to. They planned to stay in Grand Falls with their terminally ill grandmother and look after her. After that, they just didn't know where their lives were going.

A Message from Katrina

Down the line Coli went. The daze of shock was starting to wear off and people were beginning to make plans again. Those who had something to rebuild were talking about returning, but many were talking about starting again somewhere else. They were using terms like 'global warming' and 'rising sea levels' as part of their rationale for not returning. She heard a group of teenagers singing *The New Earth Song*. She remembered it from her first day back in town. The dirge-like tune reminded her of a funeral.

> Now, none of us is watching,
> As the Arctic glaciers swelter.
> Ocean levels swamp our cities,
> As our trade and commerce falter.

> Climate change affects us all,
> Oh, send the message far and wide.
> Local and sustainable we'll try,
> To combat climate change is why.
> Our future can be bright,
> If we treat our planet right.
> And we can carry on, can carry on
> Yes, we can!

Well, she hoped they were right. For every person who was going to carry on and rebuild New Orleans there seemed to be two who were going elsewhere. Like her, they had found other opportunities.

Coli set up the interviews for broadcasting. She was very busy over the next month. She spent her days working on new programs with George and getting to know what was happening in town. Late afternoons and evenings were spent with Orlando at *Big Easy Moves*. Then, if the two of them were still awake, they spent some very enjoyable time together, alone.

'Beware of what you wish for.' Right now Jubal was wondering why being the famous athlete was not enough for him. Why did he have to buy a farm? Decide to make it organic? A lot of his money was oozing away and all he had were gainfully employed friends and problems to solve. Right. That's where delusions of grandeur pushed a person. Damn, these chairs were just too short. He needed to have at least one chair in here tall enough that his knees weren't brushing his ears. Maybe he ought to make a gift of a large chair to Marilyn, partly in thanks for her hosting these meetings in her new retirement condo. Walter might like to sit in something a little more solid too.

A Message from Katrina

At least Kincaid was comfortable. He always complained that he had stopped growing too soon but Jubal bet that Kincaid never even noticed the chairs he sat in. Kincaid was such a support. He knew where everything was, how much it cost and how many more they needed. That was one person always on his side. He couldn't say the same for his father, Rev. Weekes. He supported by pointing out what was wrong with Jubal's decisions.

Walter, his farm manager, oops, consultant, and previous owner knew the farm really well. He just kept asking Jubal questions until Jubal finally got the point. Jubal's Uncle Thomas was there too. He had always supported Jubal, first with a summer job and then by building basketball hoops and a court on his farm. Finally, there was Enrico, seated across the table from him. Enrico actually made things happen. Jubal noticed that he was looking uncomfortable. Right, that meant that he needed something that he didn't think Jubal would want to pay for. Right. The sooner he started this meeting, the sooner it would be over. He cleared this throat and asked Enrico to begin.

Enrico gave his report. The crops destroyed by the storm winds had been ploughed in. The fall crops had been seeded. The market garden crops closer to the farmhouse and their Saturday market had survived in part and he really needed some more farm workers to get them harvested.

"All these people, sitting around waiting, you'd think we'd have lots of labor."

"Getting good labor was always part of my biggest headaches," contributed Walter.

"Why is labor so hard to find?" asked Jubal.

"Could be the generally low wages you offer," said Rev. Weekes. Trust his father to add a little dig, thought Jubal sourly.

"But, probably it has more to do with history," he continued. "Too many people associate farm work with slavery or share cropping."

"So, how can we change that?" asked Kincaid.

"How did you get interested, Jubal?" questioned Walter. "You could have spent your money on anything. Why my farm?"

"I guess it started the summer my parents forced me to work on my Uncle Thomas' pig and poultry farm when I was a teenager. I kicked up a big fuss and they sweetened the deal by fixing up a ball court for me to practice on. After my eight hours a day of farm labor was done, that is. I realize now that the farm work gave me muscles and the evening practices sure helped my skills."

"That's it," shouted Kincaid. He leaped up to his full, unremarkable height. "We need to advertise on the local TV. Why pay the gym fees for exercise when we'll pay you? Bends and push-ups in the bean patch will take off pounds a week."

"That would be a different approach," chuckled Walter.

"Maybe we could offer older teenagers four hours in the fields and then two hours of ball practice with me or some of the team," said Jubal. "This could work, if we were willing to have four hour shifts and called them exercise in the fresh air. We could start with some well known people in the community supporting the idea."

"Some of my congregation could certainly use the exercise," contributed Rev. Weekes.

"Whoa, this is all fine and good but I can't be ferrying workers in and out of the fields every few hours. That's too hard. The book-keeping's bad enough now," protested Enrico.

"So, you move the actual workers and I hire someone else to keep track of hours, wages and all the paperwork," suggested Jubal.

"It's crazy enough that it just might work," conceded Enrico. "It's probably better than bringing in Jamaicans or Mexicans." Rev. Weeks and Jubal looked uncomfortable. Enrico noticed and finished stiffly, "Local people would at least spend their wages locally."

Jubal was tired. He had just spent far too much time talking about farming. While in theory he knew it was important, and he knew it would be his retirement career, still, enough was enough. The meeting had just about finished him off. Now he had to learn at least a bit about compost teas, effective microorganisms, and biodynamic theories so that he could do more than simply rubber stamp their suggestions. He moved his shoulders a bit trying to get the tension out.

At least he could approve of the plan to move his uncle's extra chicken and pig manure over to his own compost heaps. Farming was more complicated than he remembered from his teenage years, but it did give him something to keep his mind going, or overheating, as it was now. He needed to float mindlessly for a while, maybe have a coffee down at the Broken Cup and do some people watching.

He chose a chair and table outside where he could stretch out his long legs without annoying anyone. At least it was getting a little cooler now with Fall in full swing. He looked up to see Doris and another woman coming out of the coffee shop. From his chair he had to look a long way up to see her face. This was definitely worth the effort. She had a big smile, lovely eyes, pronounced brows and a wild swirl of black hair. And look at that body, he thought, plenty of curves where they should be. Jubal realized that he was tired of women who rubbed their bony bodies against him without any encouragement. The two women hadn't seen him and were turning away. He'd better act fast.

"Hey, Doris," he called out.   Two pairs of eyes swerved in his direction.

"Hey yourself," Doris called back as she angled towards him with her tall, curvy companion behind her.

"You guys on your break?" Jubal asked as he racked his brains for something intelligent and compelling to say.

"Yeah, just heading back," Doris replied as she shifted her gum to one side of her mouth.   Jubal saw a lovely long elbow poke her gently in the ribs. She winced a little and said, "Right, Jubal this is Martha Lewis, who is here from New York to help get the assistance cheques to everybody. You know, she spends most of her day behind a screen tracing their references.   Better her than me," she said with a grimace.

She noticed that Martha was waiting and looking a little nervous and ill at ease. She remembered her manners and continued, "This is Jubal Weekes. He's Kincaid's boss at the farm and also a basket ball player for The Playmakers".

Jubal came back to the moment with a start.   He was amazed. Martha. He couldn't believe his luck, an old-fashioned name.   He was so sick of Tiffany, Alison and

Chelsea that he never wanted to hear another trendy name. He realized that the expectant silence meant it was his turn to say something. He tried something he thought would be safe.

"So, do you play ball too?" he asked. There was another silence while she looked embarrassed. Jubal cursed himself for assuming that every tall girl played ball.

"No, I don't follow sports," she replied. "Lots of people at school tried to get me interested but I was a computer geek, even then. Plus, I was afraid that I would be too clumsy."

Jubal tried to smile at her to put her at ease while he cursed himself. He could talk to guys but with women he had never had any practice. They were always mobbing him after the game and talking was not what they had in mind. He watched in dismay as she backed up into a chair, squeezed her coffee cup so hard that the plastic top popped off and spilled some coffee on her shirt. She hardly noticed as she said, "We've got to get back to work. Nice meeting you. Bye". She hurried away.

Jubal wasn't so busy mentally kicking himself that he failed to notice how enticingly her backside moved down the veranda steps out onto the street. She was moving so fast that Doris had to run to keep up with her.

"Wait up," Doris puffed. She saw Martha's strained face turn around to her.

"I am so embarrassed", Martha wailed.

"Why?"

"Why? You ask me why? I finally meet someone taller than me and good-looking with a nice smile and I blow it completely. I don't know who he is and I fall over a chair. Who is he anyway?"

"Girl, you really don't know?" asked Doris. Receiving a blank stare, she continued, "Even in New York there would be some sports commentary about him. You know, most baskets in least games and most games won in his career, that sort of thing. I'm not much of a sports fan either but Kincaid, who worships the ground he walks on, is educating me."

Martha moaned a little. "You have to coach me on how to talk to guys. My record so far is abysmal and I really want to get to know him,"

"We'll ask Kincaid. He used to be the team's equipment manager before Jubal got him the job of accountant for the farm."

"I thought you said that Walter was Kincaid's boss."

"Well, he is. But Walter is the farming consultant and Jubal is his boss. Jubal bought Walter's farm to begin with and is building it into something impressive."

"I certainly wasn't impressive," wailed Martha again. "Did you see how he shut right up when you told him my name was 'Martha'? I like it, but sometimes I wish my mother had watched soaps instead of studying George Washington," she groaned.

"Don't beat yourself up, Martha," counselled Doris. "He's an athlete, not a flirt. Besides, he likes to think before he talks, so he's not great on a swift repartee."

"Wow, the words you use sometimes, girl", replied Martha, feeling a bit better. Maybe Jubal was like her, and always thought of the perfect thing to say five minutes too late.

"Yeah, I read a lot", returned Doris with a grin. "Do you want to see him again?"

"I'll run into him again around town, won't I?"

"Maybe not. He's probably only here for a day or two and then he'll be back on his game schedule." Doris watched Martha's face cloud over. "Don't worry, he'll be over at Orlando's pub, *Big Easy Moves*, tonight. Put on your sex-y-ist, and we'll go on a little crawl," Doris finished with her best effort at a leer.

A couple of weeks passed in a blur of action and enthusiasm. There were just so many people in town with so many different stories and then the club after work. Coli was meeting a new group of people, people who could become friends.

It was, once again, busy that night at Big Easy Moves. Some of the people came to hear Orlando and his band play, but some of them came to talk to Coli about the news behind the news of Katrina. Other people came to talk small town politics. Coli realized for the first time, that the club was becoming an informal centre for the town and a good source of issues and ideas for her. Maybe she could put together some ideas for programs that would have local and wider interest. Maybe she didn't need a disaster to find news to interest the public.

Even so Coli was tired. She was ready to abandon Orlando and the evening. Martha, Doris and Kincaid had already left, pleading work next morning. She felt a tap on her shoulder and turned around to see Jeanne, Orlando's mama behind her. She smelled of the meal that Coli had been very happy to eat earlier. Coli stood up and Jeanne gave her a hug.

"Wow! Your hair looks really good, Jeanne."

"I went to see your Mama today, Coli."

"She did a good job." Coli smiled.

"She asked after you. Maybe you could go by tomorrow." Jeanne hugged Coli again and headed back to the kitchen. "Talk to you tomorrow when I have more time."

Her own guilt and Jeanne's encouragement pushed Coli to visit Charlene during her lunch hour the next day. She found her mama at the kitchen table in the back of *Cost Effective Cuts*. Charlene had the remains of lunch on the table and a coffee cup in her hand.

"Sorry it took me so long to see you again," Coli started with a determined smile. Charlene waved away her apologies. Coli tried again. "Tell me again how it was when you left town. I was too tired and excited to get it last time I talked to you."

Charlene sighed. "When I packed up to leave before Hurricane Katrina I could only find Ed's old duffel bag to use. I drug it out from the back of the closet. Seeing it again made me realize   some stuff." She took a drink of her coffee and looked at Coli. "It weren't so much that I didn't love Ed no more. No, more like I weren't that young girl no more."

"But you loved Dad, didn't you?" Coli hated herself for being so needy.

"Yeah, and I paid for it. I never listened to the old aunties. They used to harp on and on to us young girls. 'Don't get pregnant Charlé! Each pregnancy lasts twenty years.'   Huh," she snorted. "You can tell teenagers good stuff. They just can't hear you." She looked significantly at

Coli and took another sip of her coffee. "I'd offer you a cup but you wouldn't want it."

Coli thought her mother could at least ask her but decided not to be critical. Charlene was trying to share her thoughts and feelings. That seldom happened.

Charlene continued. "That scared young girl with her burdens. She's long gone. Her betrayed love, long, long gone. Her daughter to raise on her own—all growed up. I don't have to be her no more." Her eyes stayed on her coffee. "I'm going to be somebody better." She looked down on her coffee with distaste.

"Need your afternoon beer?" Coli regretted her big mouth as soon as she closed it. Her anger seemed to boil up from nowhere. She thought of all the times her mother had tried to quit but couldn't, not for Coli anyway. "Sorry. If you're trying to quit I'm glad."

Charlene shifted and sighed. She didn't look at Coli. "Maybe this time I can. Maybe you'll even like me better when I can."

The silence stretched between them. They watched the dust motes sift down upon the chipped coffee cup and Grace's carefully worked doilies. All those years of wasted pain.

The kitchen door was pushed open. "Good to see you, Coli," warbled Grace. "You should see your mama's new beau." She caught the mood. "Ray's a banty rooster charmer who would lighten the gloom around here if you'd only give him half a chance."

Grace marched over to the fridge, pulled out her beer, and ripped off the tab. She said pointedly, "Nice weather we're having, for an Eskimo."

Coli shifted in her chair, then stood up. "Okay, I'd be happy to meet Ray. After all, I am 'all growed up' and theoretically self-supporting. I have news to chase. Nice chatting with y'all. Bye now."

Coli was heading toward the outer door when a short cowboy opened it and looked around the room. He seemed disappointed until he saw Charlene coming in from the kitchen. He took off his hat and his eyes sparkled with joy. "You can't need another haircut. It don't grow that fast." Charlene's greeting was softened by her smile. Ray tried to look bashful.

"I was just in town to pick up a few things and thought you might like to go for drink."

"Maybe one." Coli looked a question at Charlene.

"One is better."

"Better than what?" asked Charlene mystified.

"Better than lots."

"Okay, we agree then. But I've got clients all afternoon. I won't finish until 5:30."

"That's good. I've business to see to here in town. Then, we can have that drink, or better yet dinner." Charlene nodded. "I'll see you then."

He turned to go and just about walked into Coli. "Ray, this is my daughter, Colette."

"Pleased to meet you," he said with a big smile and energetic handshake. "You remind me of someone." He looked at her carefully. "Besides your mother of course. You're both so beautiful," he finished with a wink.

"My working name is 'Coli Duncan'," returned Coli with a hard won smile. It wasn't Ray's fault that Charlene had named her Colette.

"Of course, Hurricane Katrina. You did a good job. It looked pretty bad there for a while. Glad I was at the ranch. Not as bad there but I did what I could to keep the stock in sheltered places." He smiled at her again. " I liked the interviews you did. Too bad about the coffee maker. Glad to see you recovered. Well, see y'all later." With that he turned on his heel and swaggered out the door.

"Wow, there's a force to be reckoned with," said Coli, looking at her mother in amazement.

"You reminded me before. We're all growed up here now," Charlene smiled to herself.

Coli returned to an afternoon of chasing news around town. None of it was as amazing to her as her visit with her mama.

Coli and Orlando were still breathing hard. They were wrapped around each other, snuggled into Orlando's bed. Well, the mattress on the floor, actually. Neither one of them had had time to go and see about a bed yet, not that there were a great many stores up and running, except the ones that had the basics.

Of course it was late, in fact, late enough to be considered early. Coli had had a full day and should have been ready for sleep. But, she couldn't relax because she was still torn by that phone call earlier in the day.

"Orlando?" she whispered.

"Huh", he replied sleepily.

"I've got to tell you something."

"Can't it wait?" He groaned.

"No!" She wished she had been bright enough to leave it until morning when she could see Orlando's face, but she knew that she wouldn't be able to sleep. "Best American News phoned me today." She felt Orlando become alert beside her. "Hurricane Rita is coming and they've offered me a temporary job with Roger, to cover it."

"You're going?" Orlando was wide awake now.

A Message from Katrina

"I'm considering it," Coli replied. She wanted to go but she didn't want to leave him. Butterflies of unease surged and fluttered in her stomach.

"I love you, Coli," Orlando said slowly. "I thought when you came to Grand Falls that you loved me too and wanted to stay here with me. I want you to stay here with me." He could feel her relaxing against him. " I hoped that soon I could start talking about a wedding, with or without your mama's approval. But, I want you with me. Permanently." Afraid to pull her close as he wanted to, he lay, instead, in quiet fear.

"I'm considering it," was all Coli could bring herself to say.

"I know that I gotta stay here. I need my music and my club." He sighed. "You can be a success anywhere. You can cover the disasters around the country or you could stay here and work at the local station. You could help report, and maybe even help create the politics to bring people together here to build..." He trailed off and gave into his anger and fear.

" Shit Coli, you could chase disasters forever and inform the couch potatoes until you're old and grey." He rolled over and stuffed his fist in his mouth, to stop himself from spewing more garbage that wouldn't help.

Coli slowly moved over so that they lay back to back. Wow, Orlando really could talk when he wanted to.

Most of the time he'd rather be off with his music or listening to what his friends had to say but he'd actually said that he loved her. That he loved her. Why didn't that seem to be enough? What was wrong with her? She snuggled a little closer to him, taking the physical comfort that she could from his love while her mind and stomach roiled with the decisions yet to make.

Morning did come, sooner than either of them wanted. Coli had planned to meet with Roger at the pub at 11:00. Orlando agreed and determined that he would be there too. If his presence didn't plead his case, then nothing would.

He surveyed the pub that he was so proud of. It wouldn't open until 4:00 and had the usual sad and forlorn look of a nightspot in daylight. Orlando had been so proud of his own place, but now he worried that it couldn't compete with a career in network television. He just wished that this meeting were over. He needed to play something fast and furious.

Coli came down the stairs. They heard the door open. Orlando looked up and saw a familiar, good-looking man in his forties enter and smile at them. As he came closer, Coli started the introductions: "Hello, Roger. I hope you had a good trip. This is my friend, Orlando. He's the owner of Big Easy Moves."

A Message from Katrina

"Well hello, Orlando," replied Roger. He leaned forward with a flirtatious smile. Suddenly, something always known but never acknowledged became clear to Coli.

"I'll bring us some coffee," said Orlando, coolly, with a wry look towards her. He walked into the kitchen.

Coli hissed. "He's mine, Roger, so just stop that."

"Pity," replied Roger with a non-repentant grin.

In the kitchen, Orlando made the coffee and searched around for some of last night's sandwiches. Well, that was a relief. He could dump all that wasted jealousy. At least an intimate relationship with Roger was not a factor in the equation. For either of them.

He returned with the tray in time to see Roger looking furious and Coli determined. "You're turning down a network job, after all I've done for you," Roger stormed in disbelief.

"Yes," Coli quavered as Orlando held his breath in hope. "I'm going to stay right here and work for the local station. It's just getting set up. With all the refugees already here, and more coming because of Rita, we have a lot of public service announcements to do. I can be a major player in helping to build this community."

"You mean that you're going to turn down all that money for a half or a quarter of the salary." Roger looked at Coli's set face. "What about the fame? Coli Duncan, ABN's rising young reporting star," he sneered at her openly. Then, he looked in blank astonishment at Coli and Orlando standing together.

"I got promises to keep," Coli said slowly, as if making her decision as she spoke. "I was just too afraid to say them until now," she continued with gathering confidence.

"That's no reason to stay in this one horse town. Let me know if you ever think better of this stupid decision. You'll see me on the News." He stalked out and slammed the door.

"I think I need that coffee now," quavered Coli. She noticed that her hands were shaking, "What have I done?" she moaned. "No top journalist award for me now."

"You won't need it," replied Orlando with relief. Turning her in his arms, he kissed her passionately. She kissed him back, her passion tinged with disbelief. What had she done?

CHAPTER 17

"AMBITION, THOU FIEND!"

No matter that Coli had thrown away her potential star status, she still had work to do here. Closing the back door of the kitchen, she looked at her bike, leaning against the wall. It didn't have a lock. It didn't need one. Only three gears worked and the rust had been hidden in left-over paint. Someone in the pub had mentioned a bike to give away and Orlando had been quick to organize her 'present'. Not exactly her dream car, but the gas mileage was good.

Coli cycled over to the local station. Just because she had said "no" to Roger didn't mean that she didn't have significant work here in Grand Falls. George, her once again boss, would want to see her interviews of those waiting for aid. She was surprised to see Roger's van parked outside. She hurried to the door and went inside.

"Well, if it isn't the homebody," sneered Roger. "The 'I'm staying right here with Orlando' thing, didn't last long, did it?"

Coli glared at Roger. She banked down her anger. "I am a journalist. I do work here, even if I don't reach your standards, Roger," she replied evenly.

George glared at Roger. "Covering Hurricane Rita doesn't mean that you can't come back, Coli. You did good on your first time out. Your coverage of Hurricane Katrina made me proud."

Coli turned to look at Roger and suddenly the penny dropped. It clanged loudly against her self-esteem. "You set it up, George!"

"You may be good for your age, Coli," said Roger, "but do you really think that BA News would have ever heard of you without me and George?"

"So what's the connection?"

Roger smiled. "George got me started as a hotspot commentator. I used to cover football and he was one of the few players who could string two interesting sentences together."

"With that attitude it's a wonder that you lasted as long as you did in sports reporting." George smiled at Roger and Roger returned a smirk.

"Yeah, people who know people. I'm glad you got me out of there, George," returned Roger with a widening grin.

"You never had the proper reverence for football, Roger."

"And you, Coli, don't have the proper reverence for what George has done for you," continued Roger. "Hurricane Rita is brewing out in the Gulf. It started off as the fourth most intense Atlantic hurricane ever recorded and now it's become the most intense tropical cyclone ever observed in the Gulf of Mexico. It's the fifth major hurricane this year. It could make your career."

Coli looked torn. George continued quietly, "Your job with me will still be here when it's over. It's not like you're leaving Orlando. He'll be busy boarding up the windows of the club and playing his music. You'll be back before he even notices," persuaded George.

Coli looked at George. Did men really think like this, she wondered?

"Katrina and Rita will be a one-two body blow to the city. You'll be famous as the reporter who witnessed the death of the first major American city to climate change disaster. Tah, da!" Roger finished with a flourish.

Coli felt like giving him a good kick in the shins but what he said did set her thinking. One assignment out of town didn't mean that she was abandoning Orlando. She didn't spend all day, every day with him as it was. She could do this without loving him less and he could still love her in her absence. She was coming back, after all. Unlike... no, she wouldn't go there. She looked at Roger, "How long can you wait for me to get my stuff?" she asked.

Coli jumped off her bike and dumped it at the back door of the Club. When she opened the door she could hear Orlando playing the piano. The soft music floated in the air, serene and blissful, somehow reminding her of something loving and joyful. She heard a sax come in, complementing the melody line but sounding more solid and directed. Probably he was jamming with Sol, a young saxophone player who had evacuated with little more than his sax. It made her feel that Orlando could understand her change of heart, could see that this one assignment didn't mean that she didn't love him. Surely he could see that she would be back, in fact, maybe he could write some music around Hurricane Rita. Coli could hear it in her head, clashing, violent, and remorseless.

She came into the back of the club and sprinted for the piano. Courage now she thought. Both musicians turned to her in surprise. She blurted out, "Don't be mad,

Orlando but I've changed my mind. I have to go. One more big assignment won't change how I feel about you."

Orlando looked at her in amazement. She saw his feelings cycle from disbelief, to disappointment and then to anger. He spoke slowly, seeming to hold back a torrent of words, "You go, girl. You go be famous. I'll watch you every night. You made your choice. I'll make mine." He turned away from her, and started pounding on the keys. The anger and force of the music rolled back at her. Sol looked at Coli and Orlando cautiously, frozen into silence.

Coli wished she had let Orlando give her his usual welcome home hug before she had blurted out her change of heart, but she couldn't go back. She felt very sorry for the dependent thing she had become and then she felt her own anger starting to build.

Orlando should realize that it wasn't an easy decision for her. What was wrong with him? She realized that she was pounding one fist rhythmically into her other hand. Fearing her usual explosion of anger she turned and raced for her suitcase. Better to use all that energy to get ready. Roger wouldn't wait forever and she sure didn't want him coming here again.

Coli was trying hard to block out the relentless shrieking of the storm winds. Even with her meds her head was throbbing in tune to the blasts of air. This hurricane, no Tropical Storm Rita, had one of the lowest air pressure levels ever recorded. Every migraine sufferer in Louisiana, Florida and Texas knew all about that. The throbbing in her head made it hard for her to concentrate on what Roger was saying.

"Although Rita has been downgraded to a tropical storm, high winds and rain are pounding New Orleans for the second time in less than a month. Whatever clean up has been done here, is being torn apart by the fury of nature. Although winds are high, the body blow to the city did not materialize. Instead, the storm came ashore very close to the Louisiana Texas border. Galveston has borne more of the brunt of the storm than here."

"But even here, the storm surge of seventeen feet destroyed several coastal parishes and has over-topped this section of the Industrial Canal. Its breach is about one hundred feet wide and flooding is expected to reach eight feet. Everyone has been evacuated from the parish since Katrina so there will be no further evacuation needed here."

Roger stopped speaking and started to pack up.

"You sure have a commanding and supportive TV persona," said Coli.

"You do OK with your sympathetic young thing personality too, Coli," returned Roger grudgingly. "Let's get out of here before the water gets much higher. Can you get us through this storm over to Lake Charles?"

They had several false starts and detours. The wind was throwing branches, papers, small pails and other debris of normal life around. There were piles of branches by the sides of the road that were being pulled apart by the wind. Other piles of stoves, fridges, and car parts that had been gathered by AmeriCorps were shifting and rumbling under wildly flapping tarps. This new destruction of the city weighed heavily on Coli's soul. There were no people in the city, no one to save. No positive action to take here in this continuing wasteland. Why had she ever thought that she wanted to come back?

They finally arrived at Lake Charles. They managed to get close enough to film the casino boat that had come loose and crashed into the bridge across the Calcasieu River. Coli did the commentary as Roger panned the scene. Then, it was the usual tortuous and slow retreat to their hotel. Roger stayed in the van to send out their new coverage and then he and Coli went into the lobby and joined the few gathered in front of the TV.

They watched for two hours and saw only two minutes of the coverage they had worked so hard to put together. Most of the shots were of Galveston and the southwestern parishes where the main force of the storm had been unleashed. Many areas were flooded by a combination of the heavy rains and the storm surge. People who had been unable or unwilling to evacuate were being rescued. These scenes were far more exciting than the empty and ruined landscape of New Orleans.

"If the storm slows down in the morning, we're out of here," said Roger.

"But why?" questioned Coli. "We haven't interviewed anybody yet. Don't we need to create some interest here?"

"There is no interest here. Don't you get it, Coli? It's only another storm here. This is not the hurricane of the century. It's not completely crippling this proud and historic city. Nah, it's just a big wind blowing a mess around an empty city. Nothing of interest here. The big news has moved on. That bastard Rathbone was right. He positioned himself to be where the action was in Galveston, in front of the eyes of the nation. Even when I worked with him he was a self-centred prick," Roger added viciously.

Wow, thought Coli. Sounds like there is more going on here than a disagreement between colleagues. She looked at Roger with new eyes.

" Let's get out of here tomorrow before my career completely tanks."

A Message from Katrina

The long ride home gave Coli plenty of time to miss Orlando. She had phoned last night and apologized for her change of heart. She told him how much she missed him, but he was busy dealing with the storm and the people who had shown up at the Club. It had been a very unsatisfactory call.

"Big Easy Moves," Orlando had answered the phone.

"Hi, it's Coli."

"Yeah, I caught your two minutes on the news last night. Most of the storm seems to be in Galveston."

"Disappointing for Roger and me but it does mean I should be home very soon."

"Why?"

"Roger says there's no story here. No people and everybody's already seen the Katrina devastation." Silence for several beats too long.

"I've really got to go now Coli. People need me and I'm pretty tired from all the extra work of boarding up the windows and bringing in extra supplies."

"Extra supplies?"

" Yeah, it may not be news but it's still a mother of a storm here. Some people don't want to face it alone so I've got a pub full, all trying to forget their woes. See you soon."

Before Coli could say 'I love you', he had hung up. She had sat there, in her boring hotel room trying to recapture her excitement about her career. All that enthusiasm had drained away in the empty, ruined city. Sleep was a long time coming.

The grey light of morning reminded her of the futility of her trip. She looked out of the van through the streaks of rain on the window. All she saw were the tree branches at the side of the road still flailing in the wind. The rain was hammering intermittently on the roof of the van. The major winds and rain may have missed them but it was still a storm here. Still a storm in her feelings too. How did people repair relationships? She had no practise in it and had never felt till now that she should even try.

Coli finally turned to Roger. "So, what kind of family do you go home to, Roger?"

He turned and glanced at her. "My wife and two daughters about your age."

"Really? What was all that with Orlando then."

Roger shrugged his shoulders irritably. "None of your business." The silence lengthened. "You are so young sometimes. You'll find out, if you're lucky enough to build a life with some one, that relationships are what people make them. Roger stared at the road and drove without looking at Coli. "My wife brought up our girls. I'm away a lot. She has her own life as an artist. When we're together, we're together. I don't need to justify anything to her or anybody else."

A longer silence ensued. Coli was stunned by Roger's candor. "You're right." She sighed. "Maybe my life with Orlando can be what we want it to be too."

Roger had his attention back on the road. Several trees had been cut into sections but bits were still on the road. When he didn't respond, she searched her mind for a more neutral topic. They had never really talked about much more than the storms they covered.

"Remember during Hurricane Katrina?"

"What?"

"That old age home? Riverside Rest Home? You know. We could see the corpses of the old people through the windows. What did you find out? I didn't hear any more about it."

"And you won't. It's before the courts."

"When has that ever stopped the media?"

"BA News has enough litigation on the go right now."

"Off the record?"

"That's different. Remember that bus?"

"Security for Seniors? The bus that was burning on the highway?"

"Yeah. Riverside Rest Home has two buses. One was in for repairs. The parts were supposed to arrive before the storm but they didn't. Okay, plan B. Make two trips in the same bus. The one that burned was the first run. So, it didn't come back. Then, moving the seniors from the burnt out bus by ambulance out of the city took more time."

"Bad!"

"It gets worse. The guy in charge is on his first day back after recovering from a heart attack. He is trying to find another bus. All his nurses are on the first bus. Major stress. He has another heart attack and dies. Now, there's nobody but the clients there. They are in no shape to help anybody, not even themselves."

Coli remembered the corpses and shuddered again. It really was too horrible to flash onto a TV screen.

Roger looked over at her as he slowed down for a tricky curve. "Grow up Coli, reporting it doesn't fix it."

CHAPTER 18

REPORTING IT DOESN'T FIX IT

"Two roads diverge in a wood, and I—
I took the one less traveled by,
And that has made all the difference."
Robert Frost*

Coli climbed stiffly out of the Best American News van. She reached in the back for her grip and went to the driver's window where Roger was drumming on the steering wheel. She no longer saw his action as impatience directed against her, but as his own restless energy. She smiled up at him. "I'm glad you told me a bit about your life in Chicago, Roger."

"Just between you and me, kid," he replied.

"Thanks again, glad to know my hero worship wasn't wasted."

"There's lots of ways to be famous, Coli. Maybe you could even do it from here, given the Internet and cell phone cameras." Roger swept his eyes around the scene. The painted letters, BIG EASY MOVES, stared back at him from above the door of Orlando's club. "Or maybe not," he concluded with a shrug. "Well, see you at the next disaster." Roger started the van.

Coli watched Roger and the van disappear. She turned around and looked up at the sign. I must convince Orlando to replace that with something more upbeat as soon as we can afford it, she thought. She tried the door handle. It was open. Good. She and Roger had made good time and arrived early in the afternoon. Plenty of time to fix things between Orlando and herself. Coli wanted his undivided attention, before he had to concentrate on preparing for the Club. He was probably setting up for tonight.

Funny, she didn't hear him on the piano, she thought, as she dragged her grip down the hall. She could hear voices though, as she rounded the corner and looked into the main room of the club.

What she saw made her furious. She felt the familiar wave of mind-numbing anger engulf her. "Out, out. Get out now," she muttered to herself as she turned the other way and ran. She blundered down the two steps outside the club's door. She was in a rage of pain. Abandoned again, she thought bitterly to herself. I thought he loved me and just couldn't wait 'til I got back.

A Message from Katrina

Then, her thoughts swirled to another track. I should never have left. Never. It's all George's fault. My career, bringing important news to the world. Fame and fortune. Ha! I should never have left. I wanted to find the stories of those remaining, in spite of the destruction of not one, but two major hurricanes.

Instead I end up fighting with Roger about staying in New Orleans. I should never have left. Wanting Rita to be bigger. Wanting more damage, more excitement, more TV time. Besides as Roger so clearly pointed out, reporting it doesn't fix it. Doesn't fix it. I should never have left, never, never, never! Where were my brains?

"Oh, sorry Coli". Strong hands pinned her shoulders. A giant of a man held her in place as he sidestepped her. "Great coverage on Rita. So glad it's not sending us more evacuees. Good idea to keep the city closed for a few more days." He went swiftly on his way, leaving Coli to recognize him belatedly, as one of the doctors at the Red Cross Shelter. She muttered to his back, "But so what, so what? Reporting it doesn't fix it."

She dragged her bike up from beside the door. She peddled a couple of blocks in a rage and then almost ran over Doris coming out of the drugstore. Doris stepped quickly out of her way. Coli screeched on the brakes and managed to stop. "Great to see you, Coli. At least Rita was just a big storm here." She caught sight of Coli's stricken face. "Your reporting was good," she reassured Coli. "Just, you know, like short. Not your fault but I'm glad it was just a big storm."

"Reporting doesn't fix it. Seeing it doesn't fix it."

Doris shook her head at these non-sequiturs. "Talk to you soon, Coli. Gotta go. Kincaid's meeting me for lunch." She hurried away leaving Coli alone, again.

Coli went on, not noticing much. Her thoughts kept swirling around. How could he? The minute I'm gone he's got Martha draped all over his shoulder. She waved in increasing irritation at the people who kept saying "Hi Coli" and trying to engage her in conversation about Rita. She had thought that bragging about her job would be just what she wanted. That her job really mattered but now all she really needed was someone to want her for herself.

She took a short cut behind the Red Cross kitchen. Jeanne, Orlando's mother, was just coming out the back door. She saw Coli and flagged her to stop. "Coli, good to see you." She reached up as Coli stopped the bike. Her strong arms enfolded Coli's shoulders in a loving hug. "Didn't see much coverage of Rita but your bit was good."

"Reporting it doesn't fix it."

Jeanne looked at her closely. "If it isn't reported and nobody knows, it can't be fixed either." Coli seemed lost in thought. "Some things need to be 'reported' for quite a while before anyone can figure out how to fix them," Jeanne offered in an effort to connect with Coli.

"I saw Orlando with Martha." Coli set her bike in motion again, needing to be moving before her anger built up again.

"She was probably asking him about Jubal," Jeanne called to Coli's retreating back.

Coli had to keep moving. She kept pedalling. Some branches were still across the alleys. She went around them. She kept going. Suddenly, she realized that she was in the shade of old oak trees. Her bike had taken her to Cost Effective Cuts. There it was. She wanted her Mama. She sighed in disgust with herself, but her feet still led her up the steps to the front door.

How could he? She had tried to talk to him last night. Of all the lying, dishonest ... Her thoughts trailed down. She had wanted him to say that he loved her, that he missed her, that the club and even his music weren't the same without her. Huh! She guessed not. Not with Martha draped all over him, kissing him. It wouldn't be like that when she was there. Would it?

Inside the front door she saw that Charlene was tidying up her station. "Hi, Mama," she said.

Charlene turned and smiled. "Hi Coli. You're back. It was good to see you on the news that one night. Too bad the storm didn't last a bit longer." Charlene was actually trying to be nice and interested in what Coli was doing. It felt as good as a cool drink of water. At least her Mama still cared.

"It was not as bad as Katrina, but still did some more damage, and no one is officially back in the city yet. New Orleans feels pretty forlorn and broken." Coli sighed. Her mother looked at her strangely.

"What's wrong?" Charlene ventured. When Coli didn't answer, she cast around in her mind for something that would make Coli feel better. "Uh…uh….I was over at Orlando's club, Big Easy Moves, the other night. He sure plays good."

"Don't even talk to me about that loser," shrieked Coli. She quickly put her hand over her mouth. She couldn't prevent herself from continuing. "That damn Orlando, him and Martha making out the moment my back is turned!"

"Well, you have been gone for a while," replied her mother.

"Don't you take his part, Mama," Coli hissed. "I thought you didn't like him. Wrong colour. Wasn't good enough for me. What happened?"

"I've been over to the club a time or two while you've been gone. Don't look at me like that. I only had a couple." Charlene glared at Coli and continued, "Ray said the music was good and it was the place where everybody went. Orlando seems to be the guy keeping it all together. There's maybe more to him than I thought." Her eyes traveled past Coli's face to a point behind her head. Coli turned around to see short, slight but muscular Ray in his cowboy shirt, jeans and hat.

"Hi, glad to meet you again. Remember me? I'm Ray." He gave a cocky sway to his hips, to bring everyone's attention to him. "Liked your bit on Rita. It looked pretty nasty but not as bad as Katrina." He looked expectantly at Charlene.

"Just about ready to go," said Charlene. She looked up significantly at Coli. "Ray's invited me out to see his ranch for a couple of days, Coli."

Coli was staggered. I go away for a few days and my world falls apart again. She vaguely heard Charlene suggest, "Stay here until you sort things out with Orlando."

Ray and Charlene swirled away and Coli was left alone … again. "Fine homecoming," she grumbled. Maybe I should just chase disasters instead. At least somebody appreciates me then. But Roger's voice echoed through her thoughts again, "Reporting it doesn't fix it."

"George," Coli muttered to herself. "He appreciates me. I'll go see him. He has faith in my reporting. He'll know how to fix it." She headed blindly to the door, just as Grace came in from the kitchen.

"Oh, Coli. You're back in town. Good report. Glad it wasn't as bad as Katrina. We had a real blow here and rain like you wouldn't believe." She gave Coli a hug and continued, "Charlene's right. You're welcome to stay here while she's gone and I won't have to worry about the shop."

Coli felt appreciated and warmed by Grace's hug. That's all I want she thought to herself. Why can't Mama be more motherly? She returned Grace's hug and replied, "I just need to see George first and then I'll be back."

"I'm sure you'll sort it out with Orlando. He's such a nice boy," Grace twittered as Coli shut the door.

Right. Now everybody is a member of the Orlando fan club, Coli thought sourly as she climbed on her bike again.

George wasn't too surprised to see her. He didn't even remove his feet from his desk as he leaned back to look up at her.

"Too bad you and Roger weren't assigned to Galveston like Rathbone was. Not that your stuff wasn't good," added George, after taking a quick look at Coli's face.

"No wonder you and Roger are friends," said Coli. "You seem to think the same way. Roger refused to stay any longer, once our work wasn't being rebroadcast. The attention did shift to Texas. I tried to get him to do local interest interviews with the few people who were around." Coli couldn't stop herself from glaring at George. "He said the destruction and the slowness of the cleanup were old news now and everybody wanted the new stuff. It was either leave with him or walk." Coli shrugged her shoulders.

George got up and gave her a hug. "I'm glad you're back," he said. "Now, I bet you're wanting to spend time with Orlando. Don't worry about work here today. I can keep things going by myself for a bit longer."

Coli could feel her tears welling up. Oh, no she thought. I can't possibly be going to cry. She tried to control herself but the whole embarrassing story of Orlando and Martha gushed out of her with enough angst to fill a theatre.

George looked at her in amazement. He knew better than to try to calm her or stick up for Orlando. Instead he said, "This looks serious, Coli, but you really need to talk to Orlando." George watched Coli slamming her fist into the palm of her hand. He wished he could help her more. "You need to talk to him for your own peace of mind," he said softly.

Well, she wouldn't see him tonight. She was just too mad. She headed back to her mama's apartment behind

Cost Effective Cuts. Once there she took a deep breath and let it out slowly. The she walked from the small over-crowded living room to the tiny kitchen and back, again and again. As she paced she didn't notice the frilly pink curtains over the sink or the sagging cushions on the beige couch. Step after step she paced out her anger and her fear of rejection. Each step helped. Her emotions leached away and her thinking mind returned. Finally, she was tired and knew that she could sleep. She'd go to see Orlando tomorrow. Maybe by then she'd be able to hear what he had to say.

Coli could hear music as she opened the outer door of the club. The notes sounded sad and lonely. She'd learned how to listen to jazz from Orlando. He'd explained how there were basic melodies or songs but it was how each player varied and wove his play around the basic music that made the difference. Right now Orlando's arrangements sounded sad.

He had a lot of nerve to play like that Coli thought as her anger rose again. Coli raced into the back of the club and slammed the door for good measure. Orlando turned his head at the noise and then returned to the piano keys. He played the basic rift again but this time the notes he chose seemed eager and joyful. He finished with a flourish, turned around and looked up with an expectant grin. "Glad to see you in the flesh."

"Sure," replied Coli as she crossed her arms defensively and stared angrily at him.

Orlando stopped and said quietly, "What's wrong?"

"Wrong? What makes you think anything is wrong?" shouted Coli.

"Well, maybe because you're shouting at me," Orlando returned quietly. "Or maybe because you left your stuff by the door yesterday but didn't come in."

"Oh, I came in all right."

"So, why didn't you stay?" Orlando asked gently.

"You can ask me that after what I saw?" Coli was shaken by the sound of tears, very near, in her voice.

"Look, Coli, you know I love you, so tell me what you saw that's upset you so much."

Coli couldn't believe how his quiet concern and apparent love had her wanting to collapse against him for a hug and more. She gritted her teeth and tried to say evenly, "I saw Martha and you together, making out."

"No you didn't."

"You have a secret twin living here?" Coli asked sarcastically. She shook her head to clear her thoughts. She really did want to discount the proof of her own eyes.

"You were hugging Martha."

"No, she was hugging me."

"I saw your hands against her shoulders."

"She's taller than I am. If I didn't hold her back we would have been a heap on the floor." Orlando grinned. Coli could feel herself grinning back, remembering Martha's unfortunate clumsiness.

"You were kissing her!"

"No, she was kissing me."

"What?" Coli wailed. Inwardly she cringed at how needy she sounded. Orlando must have heard it too, because he leaned forward and pulled Coli towards his chest. She couldn't believe she was allowing him to comfort her.

"Coli, I love you. Martha's not interested in me. She wants Jubal to notice her. She needed to know when he'd be back in town. Her job with the Red Cross is almost finished. Only the threat of Hurricane Rita kept her here the last few days." He released his hug as she remained stiff in his arms. "When I told her Jubal would be back in two days she hugged me. Then, I said that I had seen his eyes on her in the Club. That's when she kissed me and said, "Wish me luck". I wished her luck in a hurry. She a fair load to hold up, that girl," Orlando finished.

Coli sniffed. "Don't tell me you didn't enjoy it."

"Of course, I enjoyed her telling me about Jubal. What do you think I had to listen to before Jubal left?

"Well, you are a good listener, as you're always telling me," returned Coli.

Orlando looked hesitant and cleared his throat. "Actually, there's something I need you to listen to, Coli. Seriously listen to I mean. Don't say 'no' right away." He fumbled in his pocket and brought out a small ring case. "I really did miss you when you were gone. I love you. With this ring I pledge my love to you. I want you and me to be together." He smiled at Coli. "People who just want to tell me things can't ruin us."

"Just make sure that you listen from a distance," Coli couldn't hide her smile. She held out her hand to Orlando. He placed his ring on her finger and then patted the piano bench. Coli came closer and snuggled into his side. He gave her a tighter hug. She felt wanted and loved. He played his own version of the wedding march. It started slow, low and romantic and ended with a loving, bright flourish.

"In this life, you're gonna spend lots of time reporting. I'm gonna spend lots of time lost in my music so let's not waste our time together arguing."

He played another riff, starting slowly again and bouncing with happiness at the end. Coli leaned into him. He pounded out the last note. Orlando turned suddenly, picked her up and ran for the stairs. Surprised, Coli hung on.   She struggled out of his arms at the bottom of the stairs.

"I'm trying to be romantic here," he grunted.

"I'm trying to save your energy here," she cooed, "I've got better ideas on how to use it." She bounded up the stairs with Orlando close behind.

They burst into the bedroom. The mattress on the box springs was covered in discarded clothes and quilts. Orlando swept them aside with a grand gesture.   "J u s t pretend that you're in the honeymoon suite of Motel 6."

"It might be tidier. The bed might have legs and a headboard. We really have to get a better bed." Orlando rolled his eyes. " But this will work for now," Coli finished with her best seductive smile.

"Ah, I have missed you, star of the small screen," Orlando whispered as he hugged Coli and they helped each other remove all those pesky clothes.

Much later, Coli sighed with satisfaction. She snuggled up to Orlando's back. He seemed to be sliding into sleep. "You know what's awesome about this?"

"This, what's this?" muttered Orlando.

"You know love, and sex."

"Coli, no performance report needed, OK?"

A Message from Katrina

"Don't worry, you're the five star hotel. I'd check-in to your bed again."

"Right." She could feel him relaxing toward sleep again

."But seriously, the best thing is being with you." A slight snore answered her.

CHAPTER 19

RESETTLING AMERICA SERIES

Coli was almost awake. She stretched out her arms and legs in the bed, expecting to encounter Orlando. The fact that she didn't brought her fully awake. She opened her eyes. Rumpled sheets and a quilt came into view. No Orlando. Right, he was probably already downstairs getting ready for opening. Afternoon naps always made her feel groggy, even if they were started in the afterglow of lovely, lovely sex. She took a moment to remember and enjoy.

She would get dressed in her sexiest, maybe her v-necked, tight, red t-shirt and tighter jeans. That would keep Orlando's attention on her and not Martha, pining or not for Jubal. She wiggled into her clothes and took some time to put on make-up. Ready at last, she headed down the stairs to the pub. She heard the noise seeping up at her. Maybe Orlando had the right idea. It would be great to spend the evening with people. She pulled open the door. The room was only half full but the noise of the ball game on TV and the conversations of patrons were already building. Good. Bums on seats and hands on beers. Orlando would be pleased.

Opening the door to the pub she was surprised to see it so full already and so loud. There was Randy of Rockin' Randy's Rides bellied up to the bar. He was spewing out drunken laughter just like his diesel trucks spewed out air pollution. Coli quietly slid behind him before he turned and noticed her. At least he had a beer in hand.

Farther into the room Coli stopped and looked for Orlando. Her heart lurched when she saw him. He was sitting beside Martha, almost head to head. What a fool I was, she wailed to herself. I believed him. I dressed in my sexiest for him.

She marched up to them. She tapped Orlando on the shoulder. He turned to her, smiled and reached out to hug her onto the stool beside him. She was ready to vent a green cloud of jealousy when she saw that Martha's whole attention was riveted to the TV screen. Coli saw Jubal in the purple away uniform of the Playmakers. He was laying up a shot. It flipped onto the edge of the basket, wobbled and then swished through. Martha sighed with delight. Her eyes followed Jubal as he pounded down the court. The camera shifted to the Cougars. Number 11 was throwing in the ball to resume the game. Martha lifted her eyes from the TV and saw Coli.

"Hi Coli. Good to see you're back in town. I saw you in some Hurricane Rita coverage.. The city sure looked empty. The storm there looked worse than here."

"Yeah, it was."

"How come you're back so soon?"

"Roger decided that most of the storm action was in Houston."

"Yeah, I saw that. It did seem worse. A lot more flooding and a lot more people displaced than here. In fact, people are starting to move on or move back from Grand Falls." Martha looked around the pub. "There's Doris and Kincaid. Let's go sit in the big table by the side of the bar."

Martha grabbed her beer and lurched off the stool. Coli followed her to where Kincaid and Doris were sitting at the back of the table. "Hi's" were passed around and everyone settled in except Orlando. "I'll just do a quiet first set," he said as he left them.

The notes of music settled around them. Doris turned to Coli. "You look better tonight. What were you on about yesterday? You nearly ran me over on your bike."

"Sorry about that. I was just really upset by what Roger said. Ever since I was a little kid I thought I could really help people and be important by reporting news."

"What did he say?"

"Reporting it doesn't fix it."

"I guess that depends by what it is."

"Reporting a hurricane sure doesn't fix it. that's true," put in Kincaid.

"But people do make decisions based on what they hear in the news," Martha said. " I was talking to a young couple just today who were going to return to New Orleans. When they heard about Rita heading in they figured they would have nothing left to salvage. So they decided they needed to rent where they didn't see a levee out the window."

Doris leaned in. "I heard on the radio that the line of credit of 20 million dollars for the mayor of New Orleans is starting to evaporate. So, now he's got to lay off 3,000 city workers. That means a lot of people can't afford to go back."

"Good, maybe my job here will last just a bit longer then," said Martha.

"Talk about no jobs," chimed in Kincaid. "I heard that ninety percent of the oil rigs in the Gulf aren't working yet. That's going to cost a lot more money and time to fix."

"Do you think that this bad weather could be caused by global warming? Is what we're doing with gas and oil the main cause or not?" asked Coli.

Silence followed that question for a few seconds before the music flowed over them again. Doris popped her gum. "That's where reporting it just might fix it," she commented.

Coli realized that Doris might actually be right. Roger might actually be wrong, or at least too cynical. She would have to think more about the power of the news later.

The talk went around at their table until closing time. Coli had enjoyed the evening but she couldn't stop thinking about all she had learned since the weather conference. It seemed to have jump-started her awareness. She took another sip of her only beer and tried to remember her early reporting assignments. First, Rev. Weekes and his campaign for new levees. Then, her trip with Marc and Lucille out to the Barrier Islands. Her talk with Marie Leveau about her grandfather's death. It all wove in and out of her mind. Then, working with Roger through the two hurricanes, and all the interviews. Reporting may not fix it but knowledge was power. All of her work had to mean something. There had to be something that could be done. Something that mattered.

Coli didn't sleep very well. In her dreams she kept going over and over the events of the summer. Finally, at about 6:00 am, she gave up and went in to work. At least there she had access to a computer and as much information as she had time and energy to find. She decided that if global warming and all those extra strength hurricanes were caused by too much carbon in the atmosphere that would be the place to start looking for what to do. She googled carbon overload and found pages of references. She was drowning in all the information when George came in.

"You look better today but tired," was his opening comment.

"I sorted it out with Orlando," Coli replied looking pleased.

George smiled and refrained from saying 'I told you so'.

"I also talked over Roger's idea that 'reporting it doesn't fix it' with my friends at the pub."

"Don't take every thing he says seriously."

"We decided that it depended on what was being reported. And that if we didn't know about it we couldn't do anything about it."

"Okay…?"

"So look. Look at this George.'Building community resilience is our best response to looming economic, energy, and environmental challenges of the 21st century'. Look at all this stuff this guy Richard Heinberg* has written. Look at it all on his Post Carbon website." She turned the screen towards George.

"Can I please have a program on 'Our future: how we can carry on'?"

"Whoa, slow down. We've got today's news to cover first."

"Please, please, pretty please." Coli wasn't above a little girl's appeal if it worked. "I want to stop spending all my time reporting disasters and start spending some of my time reporting on how to 'fix it'."

"News, news, Coli".

"Just a little bit of time?"

"Maybe, if you used the 'human interest stories' space."

"Yeah, yeah. I could find people who are already doing what needs to be done. Maybe even people who are planning less carbon intense projects. Yeah, yeah, this could work."

"I'm not paying for more than four hours a week. The rest is on your own time." He could tell that Coli had stopped listening. Her eyes were glued to the post carbon website again.

"Coli?" She looked up. "Today's news first."

"Absolutely." She looked at her watch. "Lucky me, lunch break now. This afternoon I'm interviewing at the Mini-mart about the latest break-in. Then I'm on to talk to the mayor about the main issues in the next election. Hey, maybe I could ask him about his top three sustainability projects locally."

"Coli," George growled.

"Hey, y'all got to start the conversation somewheres." George looked annoyed and opened his mouth. Coli waved him to silence. "Today's news first. I'm on it."

Coli could already feel herself starting to sweat. She just wanted to finish the interview with Jubal before her crisp white shirt and navy suit jacket looked as limp as she felt. She pushed open the door into the Grand Falls Cable TV studio.

George was hunkered over one of the cameras fiddling with something. He turned and looked at her. His piercing whistle rattled her carefully maintained calm. "Well, look at you. Haven't seen that suit since the weather conference." His eyes traveled over her professional shirt and jacket and then reached her cut-off shorts. "You seem to have forgotten that really fetchingly tight skirt and the classy shoes."

"Don't need them if you've set that camera up right. We agreed on only face, shoulders and table shots. Remember?"

"Yeah, yeah. I live for the day we can hire a camera man." He looked at her again. "You look nervous. Don't know why. You did lots of interviews with refugees from Katrina and those few from Rita. You even held the camera. It only bounced around a bit, even I hardly noticed it."

A knock at the door startled George and cut off his ramblings. "Come in," he called.

Jubal ducked his head to come in the doorway. Seeing him bend down, Coli was reminded of just how tall he was. He really was gorgeous: a younger and darker version of Rev. Weekes, his father. He was wearing a purple and yellow t-shirt, the Playmakers' colours, no surprise there. The way Jubal said, "Hi, George" and gave him a high five, certainly was.

"You two know each other?" asked Coli.

"Sure, Roger introduced us one time when he was still covering sports. He said that you would make your mark on the basketball scene and he sure was right."

Jubal passed on the compliment. "I sure liked his coverage of Katrina and Rita. He made me feel better about the losses we all felt." Jubal looked at Coli. "You were great too," he added.

Coli looked at the big clock on the wall. "It's time to get seated. Did you have a chance to look over my questions?" Jubal nodded a 'yes'. They seated themselves behind the table and arranged their notes. George had them practise looking into the camera and saying their names just to help them get ready.

"This is Coli Duncan presenting 'Our Future: How we can carry on'. This is the first part of the series, 'Rebuilding small town America: A Vision of a Sustainable Economy'. A small town local and sustainable economy could be one of the ways to create a lower carbon future. In this first program of our series, I will be interviewing the people of Grand Falls, Louisiana. Grand Falls is a rural town which has struggled since WWII to retain its population and family farms as its economic base. This has been a losing struggle. In the last decade, statistics show that the average family farm income has been negative. That means farmers and their families must work at other jobs to finance 'their farming addiction' which dominates their weekends and evenings. At the present time, there are fewer farmers on their farms, than there are prisoners in jail in America. This is not a sustainable basis for a healthy American economy or life style."

Coli paused. "For more on this topic we are pleased to have Jubal Weekes with us today. We will not be talking about basketball, for a change. However, most of your interviews do revolve around that topic." Coli nodded to him. "Jubal?"

Jubal: " Well, basketball is my sport and my career. I've been very lucky to play with a great team like The Playmakers."

Coli: "That has been a lucrative career, as well as making you famous."

Jubal: "Yes, I've had to do some serious thinking there."

Coli: "And what did you decide?"

Jubal: "I wanted to invest my money in America and the American people."

Coli: "But farming? Most people don't see that as a good investment."

Jubal: "The Farm College was my first investment, but since then I have diversified. Now, I'm into condo and apartment construction and small business loans here in town."

Coli: "What led you to invest in Grand Falls in the first place? This town has been barely alive for decades."

Jubal: "Well, I used to work summers for my aunt and uncle at Pineridge Farm. They raised organic chickens, turkeys and pigs just outside of Grand Falls. My uncle was always on about the need for more family farms for a strong and sustainable America. Then, a few other events brought the vision together. At the time, my father was organizing one of the first urban exodus groups. His parish in New Orleans was below sea level and only protected by aging levees."

Coli: "Hadn't Rev. Weekes been very active in a campaign to upgrade the levees?"

Jubal: "Oh, yes! He had been trying for about fifteen years to convince politicians that it was a priority. Many of them agreed with him. Other projects seemed to receive funding but all he got was promises. He finally decided that promises weren't good enough. Even before Hurricane Katrina, many scientists were predicting that global warming would produce higher sea levels. My Dad knew that this would mean disaster for his parish."

Coli: "I remember covering a media event he organized to highlight the need for better levees. Did you see it?" Jubal shook his head no.

Coli:"His church choir was arranged on risers. The choir members on the bottom two risers were costumed as fish. Hurricane Katrina showed us that he was pretty accurate in showing how high the water would be. So, he was right about his parishioners needing somewhere else to live. In fact, I went on a bus trip with my mother and other members of his congregation to see Grand Falls early this summer. So, you're not worried about renters or buyers for your condos?"

Jubal: "No. We have Dad's parishioners. Add to that group, workers in 'The ShoesToWalkOn Paving

Company'. Then there's people able to work from home due to technology and those leaving the big cities to retire. I think we have the potential for a thriving community!"

Coli: " 'ShoesToWalkOn'? What's that?"

Jubal: "It's a new recycling factory. They plan to grind up old sneakers, mix them with asphalt and use them for walkways and wharf surfaces. I hope it works out for them."

Coli: "I certainly will try to bring them in for a later interview here at our local cable news program, 'Our Future: how we can carry on'. We go now to our advertisers who are bound to be a big part of that future."

Coli saw George turn the recording light from green to red and knew that he was sending out the pre-recorded commercials. She turned to Jubal. "I didn't know that you knew all that stuff. You usually just talk about your basketball plays and scoring."

Jubal gave her his slow, shy smile and said, "I'm usually only asked about my basketball plays and scoring. I don't really know the details about all this stuff, but I know how to hire people who do. Kincaid is pretty smart under all that hair. For your interview, I cheated by cramming with him and my uncle. They talk about this stuff endlessly. My uncle always says he has lots of time to think when he's on the tractor or mucking out stalls. He says that we are going to have to rethink the idea that bigger is better. That idea gave us multi-national corporations, global trade and global warming. Now, all you hear is, 'sustainable, organic, and local'. He says that if we could make these changes our future could be protected."

"I didn't know that your uncle was such a pessimist," replied Coli.

"He views himself as an optimist," Jubal said with a sad smile.

Coli looked up to see George motioning that the advertising sequences would be over in thirty seconds. She turned to Jubal. The red light turned green and she asked him, "Your uncle has been farming locally for some time."

"Yes, I worked in the summer holidays for him. He was producing organically grown chickens, turkeys, and hogs long before it became fashionable. You should consider asking him about his experiences over the years."

"More ideas to consider in later programs of "Our future: how we can carry on. Our first series is—Resettling America: A Vision of a Sustainable Economy". See this interview on our web site www.grandfallscablenews.net. Look for our heading R4C. That means Resilient Communities Combat Climate Change. Make your comments and suggestions there. Let's get our community building a sustainable economy and future." Coli smiled into the camera one last time and watched the light change as George plugged in more advertising.

Jubal unfolded himself from his chair and turned to go. "Thanks, Coli, that went better than I thought it would." He smiled at her and headed for the door. Then, he checked his stride and turned back to her.

"You ever hear of 'Transition Towns'*?"

Coli shook her head. Jubal continued. "Kincaid was telling me about it. Look online. I think the movement started in Britain. It's about how to get from now to local and sustainable. You know what can be done at the town level to transition. Your R4C reminded me. Their web site talks about building communities that are resilient to the challenge of peak oil and climate change. Resilient Communities Combat Climate Change. Yeah, that's exactly what Kincaid was trying to get into my head. Yeah." He clearly felt that he had done enough with his suggestion. Opening the studio door and ducking his head he made his escape from stardom.

Later, as Coli was editing the interview she thought about Jubal's vision of the future. 'Local, organic and sustainable' should all help to shrink the carbon footprint, so maybe there was a chance that global warming and the extreme weather events that she kept seeing in all the media could slow down and settle down. She yearned for the steadier weather of her childhood.

Coli looked around her work space—a messy desk, an old computer, a pathetic hand held camera on the floor against the wall, no window. It was the quintessential cheap rent at a failed retail in the failed mall. At least things could only get better. In spite of her surroundings she felt energized. She felt as if she was doing something important.

She looked down at her list of local leaders. She had to interview Rev. Weekes about his vision for his church and for the town. She'd probably need to talk to the mayor and the sheriff as well. Then, she should talk to some people who had been here for a while like Grace. She could add to the interviews of some of the newer evacuees who were planning to stay, like Kincaid and Doris. She smiled to herself. She could find lots of interest without relying on the disasters that Roger seemed to need.

The club was nearly full again tonight. Orlando was playing his guitar. He didn't do that very often, although Coli liked to listen to him practising on it. He said it was better for country than jazz. The audience was actually singing along with him as if he were Bob Dylan. The New Earth Song brought that out in people.

Everybody seemed eager to sing away their grief and pain.
She listened to the jumble of voices.

       When snow storms hit the orchards,
        Oranges and lemons froze.
        Many died in icy crashes,
        And insurance costs, they rose.

       When the tornado hit our new house,
        Fifteen seconds changed our day,
        Left our home as blasted litter,
        And a mortgage still to pay.

       Each crisis gives us pain,
       But shows us lessons for our gain.
       Our future can be bright
       If we treat our planet right
       So we can carry on, can carry on
       Yes, we can!

That part at the end gave everybody a little bit of hope at least. She saw Kincaid, Doris and Jubal sitting at one table and decided to join them.

"I liked your interview on Jubal and the farm," said Kincaid. "Pull up a chair and join us," he continued. "That one's for Martha. She'll be back soon."

A Message from Katrina

Coli pulled up the chair near Martha's, but not too near. "Are those farm ads working?" she asked Kincaid.

"I've had some calls and I've also urged Rev. Weekes to bring some of his congregation. We're going to try to get some people out to harvest the veggies for the farmers' market. Another storm is coming in, and there's still a lotta of crop out there."

Jubal looked at Coli. "I got some teenagers to come out for a morning shift, lunch at the Farm Restaurant and an afternoon of ball." He remembered his interview. "Hey Coli, why don't you and your camera come too?"

He looked around and saw Orlando advancing to their table with Martha in his wake. "Hey Orlando, if you came out too it would really help to change people's attitudes to farm work," Jubal finished up. He couldn't stop his eyes from roaming all over Martha. He sure hoped her smile was for him.

Coli was watching Martha's smile with relief. Martha didn't even seem to notice Orlando as she sat down. Her eyes were only for Jubal. Then she noticed Coli and looked her way.

"Glad to see you, Coli," she said. "I sure like your 'Our Future' Program. I saw it today on my break. Wow! 'The Resettling America Series', especially the interview with Jubal was a great start." She leaned towards Coli, and said very quietly, "And you're so lucky to have Orlando.

He listened to me when I was going on and on about Jubal. Honestly, sometimes I think I don't have any pride left." She suddenly looked like she had said too much and was embarrassed. She reached for her glass of wine and picked it up awkwardly, spilling it all down the front of her light blue t-shirt. She looked at it soaking into the fabric. "I've got to go. On my last night here, too."

Doris looked up, "I'll go too."

Martha waved her offer away as she tried to get up. Her foot caught in the chair leg and she stumbled against Jubal, almost knocking him out of his chair. She cringed with embarrassment. "I'll be fine. I just need to get home," she muttered.

Jubal caught her in his arms and stood up to steady her. "Your last night? Why?" he asked.

"My job with the Red Cross is done now."

An idea was starting to develop in Jubal's mind. "What exactly did you do there?" His arms were still around Martha, but she didn't seem to be drawing back.

"I kept track of people. You know who had been paid what, where people were from, where they were going, who they needed to get in touch with. I'm good on lists and spread sheets but almost everybody who doesn't plan to stay here is gone now and so is my job." She looked up into his eyes with regret.

A Message from Katrina

"I'll walk you home so you can change your shirt and then we'll come back for another drink. I've got an idea for a job right here in town, if you want to stay," Jubal finished. Martha leaned away but her smile beamed across at him.

"Sounds good to me", she said as she reached for her bag.

Coli watched Jubal and Martha leave with relief. Her gaze floated across to Orlando who had set aside his guitar and was heading for the piano. The noise of table talk had risen again. Coli was suddenly very tired. It had been a long and exciting day. She looked around the table. Doris and Kincaid were huddled together, locked in a serious talk.

"Mind if I join you?" Coli turned to see Randy approaching the table. Oh, no. He shambled closer, sweating in his rumpled suit. His tie was loosened and he seemed ready to relax into the evening. Coli tried to beat down her dislike of Randy. Maybe it was his salesman at all costs demeanour. Maybe it was the fact that he sold the biggest, loudest trucks at Rockin' Randy's Rides. However, he was putting his bum on the chair and he did have a beer in his hand. You owe me for this, Orlando, Coli thought.

Kincaid looked up. He glanced at Randy and then at Coli. He gave Doris a quick look. He sidled closer to Randy.

Randy smirked at Coli. "No disasters to chase lately?" He gave her a look of disdain. "I didn't see much of you at the Rita coverage. Man, that hurricane sure wiped out Galveston."

"There's another storm coming into town tomorrow or next day," said Kincaid, neatly cutting off what Coli might have said. "That's why we're trying to get extra community help in getting in some crops before they're flattened. Want to come out and help."

"Whoa, not me. I've got a business to run."

"Ever think that business might be causing some of these storms," Coli couldn't prevent herself from adding.

"Huh?"

"You know. Big trucks. Big fun. Big gas consumption, often diesel. Big carbon in the air. Big global warming. Big storms." Coli felt Orlando's hand on her shoulder.

"Coli, could you give me a hand in the kitchen for a minute or two?" Orlando smiled at Kincaid, Doris and Randy. Oh no, thought Coli. Orlando of all people knows that I would be no help to anyone in a kitchen. He tugged her hand and walked with her out to the hall. "Customers, Coli," he whispered as he ushered her towards the kitchen.

"I know, I know," Coli replied as he opened the door and walked her through the kitchen to the back door. Jeanne, Orlando's mother, looked up from a sandwich she was putting together. At his head shake she returned to her work.

"Good." Orlando had backed Coli up to the wall and encircled her shoulders with his arms. "Coli, mostly I listen. Mostly, I like that but now I need you to listen." Coli fell into his compelling gaze. "He will be one of the last to buy a small electric car."

"True, hard to imagine."

"Until he does, I need him buying a beer or four at my club. So, can you turn it down a bit?"

Coli felt a surge of anger starting to build. She tried to hold it back. She gritted her teeth. "Ok," she managed to get out. She pushed her anger back again. "I'll start by working on more proactive types."

" Good, Bums on seats and hands on beer. You know my mantra." Coli nodded yes.

"So, can you go out there and be agreeable?"

Coli tried to smile but couldn't. "I don't think so."

"For me, please."

"I think I need to go outside and bay at the moon for a bit."

"Really?" Orlando looked at her with concern.

She waved her hand in dismissal. "Just give me time for a couple of laps around the parking lot and I'll recover my customer manners." She tried to smile and opened the back door.

Coli started to walk. At least it was a moonlit night. The storm clouds showed no sign of building up yet. The parking lot was full—too many big trucks. She started walking around the edge of it. The subdued noise from the bar escaped each time the door opened. She walked around once, then twice, then a few more times. She wasn't actually thinking, more like just walking off her dislike of Randy and his ilk. A few more times and tiredness started to creep up. Maybe she should just go up to bed. It was late after all.

Coli heard steps in the dark and then a giggle. She turned and saw Jubal and Martha in the street light, returning to the pub. Martha wore a new yellow and purple Playmakers t-shirt. Both she and Jubal wore even bigger grins. Coli felt happy for them.

Jubal caught sight of Coli. He came over and gave her a hug with his free arm. "I liked our interview when I watched it on-line. I got to thinking about something that Walter, my, you know, farm consultant was telling me the other day. Apparently a professor at Oregon State University has done some research on aerated compost tea."*

"Compost tea? Worms included?" Coli was vaguely nauseous at the thought.

Jubal grinned and then laughed. "Not for human consumption." He laughed again. Martha looked mystified.

A Message from Katrina

"You mix compost with water, yes. Then you bubble oxygen through it. Then you spray your soils with it. Her research shows that it is the cheapest and fastest way to go from conventional chemical farming to organic." Jubal noted the puzzled looks on Coli's and Martha's face. "Walter knows all the grisly details about which micro-organisms it feeds. You really need to talk to him."

He took Martha's hand and headed for the pub. "You coming in now?"

"I think I will head up to sleep. It's been a long day. Tell Orlando that I've gone to bed," Coli called out to them.

CHAPTER 20

SHRINKING THE FOOTPRINT

"One must begin in one's own life the private solutions that can only in turn become public solutions" Wendell Berry*

Coli was totally relaxed and still completely exhausted. In the Club last night Randy had not come in and she had not been angry. Instead, the talk had gone on and on. One idea sparked another. The last three months (was it only three months?), since Hurricane Katrina had been packed with a lifetime of changes and challenges.

She had collapsed into bed after a stimulating evening of ideas. Tired, she had hoped for restful sleep. No such luck. Her dreams brought her back to all that overload of excitement and fear. Scenes of standing in the wind and rain in New Orleans during Katrina rose up vividly. She felt the gusts of wind in her hair and the rain sheeting down on her. Then, in the way of dreams, she was shouting at Roger in his van. Then, she was boneless, asleep in the dark with a bee-no a fly-buzzing around her. She wondered what that annoying noise was. She made a huge effort to pull herself up from sleep. Right, the alarm, she thought. Her hand snaked out from under the covers and slapped the snooze button. She could hear Orlando's quiet snoring. He was not a morning person. The talk and music really had gone on far too long last night.

Sleep, sleep , her body urged but her mind was awake and active. She kept circling around all the ideas that had been talked about and the projects that she was working on for the local cable station.

Suddenly the alarm rang again, startling Coli out of bed. She shook Orlando on the shoulder and said, "Good morning. Rise and shine. Community support team today. Remember, the storm's coming and the crops are still in the field." Orlando rolled over and pulled the covers over his head. Coli tried again. "I'm going to shower and then make coffee for us to take on the Farm Shuttle." He said nothing but curled into a defiant ball on the mattress. Looking at him reminded Coli that they still hadn't gone shopping for a bed frame. Well, they didn't have time to do it today, not with those storm level gusts of wind arriving later in the day and the whole town on alert. She had a lot to do. She'd better get started.

Coli felt better after her shower. She put on her oldest and most comfortable clothes and shoes. Then, she approached the lump on the bed. She said gleefully, "Remember this was your idea. I believe you said last night in the Club, 'Put your money where your mouth is.' Only in this case, it might be put your muscle where your mouth is." She grabbed the bed covers and pulled them off Orlando. He let out a roar of outrage while she sang out: "Coffee in five."

The sun was just clearing the houses and nearby trees, its rays straining through the fast moving tatters of clouds. Coli and Orlando were propped up against the benches outside the Timothy Weekes Auditorium. The congregation had been busy. A new coat of blue paint with brown trim brightened the former warehouse. The cross by the door with 'Welcome to the Baptist Church' printed clearly below it let everyone know that it was now a place of worship. The benches outside were pure genius, especially as this was the main stop for the Farm Shuttle Bus. The bus was already here but the farm workers were straggling in. There was a group of six wiry and muscular women dressed in comfortable shoes, old jeans and loose, colourful shirts. The wind was already tugging at them, shirt-tails flicking this way and that like flags. At least the wind cooled the air a bit, but reminded Coli that the storm was coming. She reached into her bag for her tape recorder. Maybe she should interview them now. She checked her camera and went toward them.

She was coming up behind them when Martha banged into her. "Sorry," she muttered and then she turned her head and saw Coli. "Oh, it's you. Glad you could come." She seemed to remember something. "I read something you might be interested in." She gripped her clipboard and peered over her glasses. "You know, for an article or series or something." Coli nodded for her to go on. "Yeah, um Gayle Hutchinson, no Higgins, no Hudgens, that's it. Um," Martha squeezed her eyes shut to aid her memory.

"Yes, now I've got it—A. Gayle Hudgens, PhD."* She smiled with the delight of someone who has just had the right name pop full blown into her mind's eye. "And the title was," eyes closed in memory again, *Collaborative Spunk*."

"Collaborative Spunk?" echoed Coli. "Sounds a little different."

"It is a little different and it's good. It's about how to revive the people in your community to make it more sustainable and resilient. She might even come for a conference". She smiled brightly and staggered over Coli's foot. "It also talks about The Natural Step Program* that's

253

being done in Sweden. Got to go. Talk to you later." She straightened herself up and headed toward Jubal who had just arrived with a gaggle of teenagers. They were, of course, talking loudly and shoving each other.

Jubal's dad, Reverend Weekes, came out of the church and hurried down the steps. He, too, headed right for Jubal. Coli thought, ah, this could be interesting and headed that way behind Martha. She hurried over through a chorus of "Sorry" and "Oops". She arrived in time to see Rev. Weekes in consultation with Jubal.

"It could work," he insisted. "My parishioners could do with the exercise and the organic produce would improve their health. It wouldn't cut into your profits that much if they sold their extra at the Farm Market."

"Dad, Dad, I said I wasn't against the idea in principle—but leave it 'til later. We have to get the beans picked before the storm or there won't be any profits. It takes money to finish the condos for your parishioners." Jubal tucked Martha close to his side. She staggered a little and then snuggled in. "You saw the plans. The courtyard in the middle of the four condo blocks is set up to have garden plots as well as a sitting area."

"All right, but you know me. I'll keep after you until it's finished."

A Message from Katrina

Jubal tightened his lips and tried to appear supportive. He turned to Martha, "Do you have the lists of who's going where?"

"Yes, I put an experienced picker with each of the community support groups so they can be shown exactly how and what to pick. We don't know how much time we'll have."

Coli turned away and headed for the group leaders to hear their views on being teachers today. She was almost there when someone she should know hailed her. "Coli, I heard you were going to do a series on sustainability at the local level. Ever hear of 'Transition Towns'?" Coli turned, looking puzzled. She seemed to remember someone else mentioning Transition Towns, but not this person. She should know him. Suddenly it came to her. Of course, he was Gerard McInnis, the third generation owner of the Grand Falls Hotel. She smiled at him.

"Oh, hi Gerard. What's this about Transition Towns?"

"Check it out online. They talk about how to lower the carbon footprint of your town. We could have an organizing conference at the hotel. Let me know what you think." He waved at Coli. She followed after him. She really did want to talk to their group leaders in the field, and see how they felt about their new roles.

Jubal called out, "Let's go! Everybody on the bus. Martha will sort us out at the field. All aboard!"

Coli had just panned the group of teenagers going into The Farm Restaurant with Jubal. What a good idea to feed them there. Teenagers were always ready to eat. She would suggest using some of her shots in the advertising for the restaurant. Her boss, George, would be pleased. His constant mantra was 'more advertising'.

Her arms felt ready to fall off from holding her camera. She had enough shots to make a full-length feature film. All of the teenagers had wanted shots of muscled shoulders and arms at work. Most of the adults didn't want to be shown in their work clothes and bulges of extra flesh. Somehow she had kept everybody smiling and the comments positive. But she still ached in muscles she had forgotten having. If she never moved again, it would be too soon.

Orlando was propping himself up on the wall beside her. He wasn't moving that fast either. He moaned. "How did my ancestors do it? The cotton fields all day. I only did a four hour shift and I'm so stiff that I can barely move."

Coli replied, "My Cajun relatives were obviously in better shape than I am." She moaned, "At least, we get paid." They had both taken their wages, half in cash and half in farm credits. With all the fresh beans they had picked, their appetites were raging. Coli made an effort to straighten up. "I'm so hungry! Wow, it all looks good."

" Let's have lunch and then we can go and buy some of those fresh beans we picked for supper." Coli felt she would still be really hungry at supper time. She had a lot to do before the storm. She would need at least some photos and interviews, some before, during and after, depending on how bad it was. If her coverage was good enough she could urge George to send it to network news.

The daily menu on the chalkboard by the restaurant door did look good. It wasn't a lot to choose from but everything was organic, seasonal, and local. Best of all, most of it was from The Farm itself. Coli and Orlando walked slowly inside. "At the station this afternoon I have to start broadcasting our loop, *How to Prepare For the Storm*. While it's on I can edit this morning's film," she said.

"I need to organize a few emergency measures for the Club, too, before that storm arrives," replied Orlando. Then, I need to get a few hours sleep just in case the storm is not that bad and we can open. I hope that Enrico Mendosa can get the last Community Support shift out of the fields before the storm strikes."

Orlando opened the door to the restaurant. Enticing odours swirled out. The smell of food made the morning's work seem more worthwhile. What could be better than supporting your community farm? Eating good food was one of the major pleasures of life.

EPILOGUE

2045

My father rode a camel. I drive a car. My son flies a jet airplane. His son will ride a camel.*

CHAPTER 21

RIDING THE CAMEL

Duncan Weekes looked at the final version of the last video in his thesis presentation with satisfaction. After so many hours spent in virtual reality, reading and researching all that data, he was finally ready to share the finished version. Fame and fortune would soon be his... Yeah, right. Everybody wanted his take on the years since Hurricane Katrina. The massive storm had made most Americans fear that climate change had arrived in North America. Extreme weather had been biting Americans again and again ever since.

He ran his fingers through his curly black hair. His mama often said that children were more like their grandparents than parents. She had been the only one to get her Grandma Charlene's fine, curly, dark brown hair from unknown French ancestors, but he had his black explosive hair straight out of Africa from three of his grandparents.

A Message from Katrina

His dark skin, strong features and towering height were courtesy of his Grandpa Jubal, but he had missed out on his grandpa's athletic grace. Nope, he just had Grandma Martha's clumsiness. Grandpa Orlando's musical abilities hadn't come his way either.

Good thing he had Grandma Coli's curiosity. Otherwise he couldn't have kept asking all the questions and doing all the research represented in his thesis. He heard a quiet whirring from under his desk. Bending over, he banged his head as he folded himself under the desk to remove the vacuuming bot which had wedged itself between one side of the desk and the wall. Oh Grandma Martha, he thought, as he grabbed it, and backed out carefully.

He set the vacubot on the floor where it could continue cleaning. If it got stuck in another corner he would have to reprogram its sensors. But that would be later. Right now, he needed to pop back into VR while some of his allotment remained for the day.

The government may say that we have enough ambient power for all our Virtual Reality needs and desires, if we are reasonable, thought Duncan. Hence, the Ambient Power Allotment Program. Their logo was 'Ambient Power for all'*. Near the bottom of the screen in small print the asterisk was seen again. * within your allotment rating. Just plain old rationing, its opponents claimed. By careful use and family pooling for Family News Time he had barely been able to stay within his allotment. Whew!

Funny how most people now just accepted the federal agency, Ambient Power, which had centralized the use of all power sources——gas, oil, and electric. After years of destructive storms and the painful decade of the Urban Wars, a great deal of power had been needed to rebuild and resettle the survivors. Everyone accepted that a new federal grid had to be created. Also, new technology allowed more people to produce some of their own electric power from solar or wind. That went to offset their ration for household use.

Grandma Coli made sure their own solar electric power went for the lights, stove and fridge. Then she encouraged the family to pool their ambient power allotment. In fact, his grandma might be the last human to actually stream WiFi news through her TV. She insisted on a group family watching of news every night, all viewing the same thing at the same time. How crazy was that! However, it did leave more power for his research.

His allotment was only Level Four. What he wouldn't give to have a higher priority for energy use! Level Four galled his pride. It was, after all, labeled as RESEARCH—NON-ESSENTIAL. He wanted to be Level Three, RESEARCH—ESSENTIAL, like the climatologist researchers. If only his work could be recognized as significant enough! He might even be able to attain Level Two—NATIONAL IMPORTANCE.   Level One— NATIONAL SECURITY may have had an unrestricted energy allotment, but, probably contained information that someone would want to kill you for, so that didn't appeal to him much.

Duncan was very glad to have finally finished his thesis project, *The Resettling of America in Small Towns, a Major Contribution to a Sustainable Economy*. It had been a big job. Good thing that he had been able to quote from his grandmother's interviews over the years. Her cable series, *Discovering Small Town America*, was now so famous that her name had become a household word.

It sure sucked to have such famous grandparents! Everybody knew Grandpa Orlando from the Big Easy Moves Club, and Martha and Jubal Weekes were almost royalty in this small town.   So much was expected from him and then if he delivered they'd shrug their shoulders and say, "Must be easy for you with your family."

Well, this thesis project was his and his alone! Okay, maybe he did discuss it with his Grandma Coli. You couldn't overlook her work of decades, even if she was your grandma. Of course he had relied on some of her research from the beginning of the century, especially the eyewitness account of Hurricane Katrina. However, he had used the work of many others, year after year, right up until now. He felt all of it supported his thesis, but of course, he was biased.

He blinked back into VR and started to scan his thesis one last time. He heard the 'ting' of company calling. Yup, it was Theo, or T'misau, from Haida Gwaii. His avatar today seemed to be based on a Current Reality image. Strong Haida face—high cheek bones, straight black hair. His goofy smile masked a razor sharp mind. Duncan blinked to the Avatar and said, "Hey, Virtual Buddy, where y'at?"

Theo replied, "Home in Massat, of course. Have you shared your thesis yet? Ambient power was good here all yesterday. I blinked share and mine was gone. Can't change it now. All I got to worry about is my defence next week." His avatar shifted again. "Isn't yours due today?"

"Yeah," said Duncan. Then Theo was off again.

"I pity you. Level Four here was cancelled until at least tomorrow. Probably a heavy use at government levels. That stand-off in the Arctic was probably gulping down electric surplus. I'm barely getting by on my power allotment."

"I'm hanging in with mine so far today and should have enough to share."

"Anyway, must be nice to be done, golden boy. Coli Duncan's grandson. How much of your thesis did she write?"

A Message from Katrina

Duncan tamped down his anger with an attempt at humour. "Virtual pistols at dawn for that remark."

"Sorry I couldn't resist, even though I know better. Try being the first born of this generation in the hereditary chief's family." Theo rolled his eyes.

They both heard Coli's voice echoing up the stairway. "Duncan, are you there?"

"Yes, grandma."

"Who are you talking to?"

"Theo, from Haida Gwaii."

"Good luck on your thesis, Theo." Coli had raised her voice further to be heard. "Talk to me when you're done, Duncan", floated up the stairs.

"Too bad nobody flies much any more. I wouldn't have minded talking to your Grandma in person about how she created the R4C movement in 2006."

"You know that scientists had been researching how increasing carbon levels in the air were causing global warming as early as the 1970's."

"Sure, hasn't everybody watched Al Gore's 'Inconvenient Truth' videos?"

"Although lots of other people were providing input on the situation, few people had any idea how to combat global warming in the beginning. Somehow the slogan 'Resilient Communities Combat Climate Change' helped people see that they could do something. They could get closer to their food supply. They could be more self-sufficient and sustainable. They could get by without 80% of the stuff in the now obsolete big box stores. Grandma Coli was pretty active in local politics in the early part of the century." Duncan couldn't help feeling proud of her.

"We're so isolated here that we have to be pretty resilient and self-sufficient too. But the thing that I emphasize in my thesis is that we have had to be defiant as well. When the multinationals were destroying our forests and landscapes for corporate profits we had to put up blockades. My elders say it was pretty scary to be staring down the grill of a logging truck, even with linked arms and drum beats."

Duncan decided to be devil's advocate. "Didn't you get jobs and prosperity out of that?"

"A handful of jobs for a few years. It didn't even come close to paying for the destruction. Times were really hard in the 20's and 30's, waiting for the salmon to return and the forests to begin growing again. Good thing we kept them out of the southern islands. That involved a major stand-off and the support of our international friends. But it's all there in my thesis. You're on my share list after I defend it. Wish me luck!"

They both heard the ominous bleat of five minutes left of Duncan's allotment. "How come you've still got power left?" he asked Theo.

A Message from Katrina

"You know all those videos on our web site, 'Drone by Haida Gwaii'?"

"Yeah, yeah. I loved your last ones on the Orca whales. I couldn't have had a better view if I had been there in person."

"A couple of decades ago, people stopped flying in as tourists. They began to use Virtual Vacations instead. Our council decided to make drone videos of our local beauty—the forests, the ocean, the whales, the salmon. We made them interactive and charged a modest pay-per-view but had millions of viewers over time. We earmarked that income for green power and infrastructure. So, now we have wind and solar power for electricity. We haven't had to do as much rationing on the Ambient Power Grid as you do."

Another bleat interrupted Theo. "Gotta go. Talk to you again soon. Good luck."

"Duncan, are you coming down soon?" Coli's voice rolled up plaintively from downstairs. Always impatient, that was his grandma, thought Duncan as he gathered himself up.

"Coming!" He blinked out of VR into Current Reality and hurried to the hallway.

Jacqueline Swann

Duncan walked past the open door of his grandparents' bedroom. The mattress and box springs were on the floor where the bed should have been. It was some kind of family joke, but he really didn't get it. He charged down the stairs and skirted his Grandma Coli who was blinking out of VR and refocusing her sight on him.

"Grandma, what is that story about your bed?" asked Duncan who had been wondering about the details for years.

"Hmm," she replied as she swung around to look at him. "The bed? The mattress works fine. Your Grandpa and I were always too busy doing other things to agree on a bed or go shopping for one. After a while it sort of became a joke. We were too busy doing more important stuff. Although some days I don't know why I bothered. I had to blink out now to save some of my allotment. I think the whole family should view the forum together."

"Which forum?"

"You know, 'The Watershed Event for Climate Change Acceptance in North America'."

Duncan sighed with impatience. His grandma never did give up. "You know I think you're wrong, Grandma. I think it was the slow build-up of events, not just one event, that made climate change an economic issue."

"You weren't there," snorted Coli. "Hurricane Katrina forced a lot of people out of their homes. That

268

happened to all four of your grandparents. Then, six weeks later, Hurricane Rita did more damage. Most of the people in New Orleans who had their homes destroyed didn't return. In the end, they defaulted on thousands of mortgages."

His Grandma continued in lecture mode. "That started the ball rolling for the deflation of the housing bubble four years later, and helped create the beginning of the New Depression in 2008. Then, in 2012, Hurricane Isaac did even more damage and broke some of the levees again."

"The news reports kept treating each event as a one-off, or a one in a hundred year event."

"Right. Every tornado, hurricane, and flood. All those massive rain storms, dust storms and fire storms. Disasters were way too frequent to be hundred year events. So much infrastructure was destroyed that we couldn't afford the repairs. Add to that the lost decade of the Urban Wars…"

Coli stopped suddenly and looked stricken. She carried the same look of grief that all adults had when remembering that time, and quickly returned to the previous topic. "Remember, Puerto Rico never really did recover from Hurricane Maria." Grandma was really on a roll thought Duncan.

"Then governments started borrowing money from China and buying more off-shore goods. Factories here closed down and so did our economy."

"But, Grandma, all the history reports from that time say that the economy recovered."

"Only economists talk about a jobless recovery. Everyone without a job knows a lie when they hear one."

" Well, there were a few other problems that weren't climate related, weren't there?"

"Such as?" Coli challenged.

Duncan's mind went blank. He wondered how his grandma could always make him feel young and brainless."Well, the wars in the Middle East and Far East didn't help.   Then, when the Dubai construction bubble burst, the global economy started to crumble. Gas and oil prices made offshore factories less competitive.   It was a whole bunch of things coming one after the other for the last four decades that got us here." Duncan fizzled out and pointed at the blank screen of their antique TV which his Grandma used a VR streaming platform for after supper Family News Time.

"So you don't agree with the former governor of California? He claimed the watershed event was when California went bankrupt after twenty years of drought and major wild fires."

A Message from Katrina

"It wasn't a watershed event. It was the culmination of dry year after dry year. The continuing drought meant big agriculture was draining all the rivers and underground aquifers. Forest fire after forest fire didn't help either," Duncan insisted.

"So you wouldn't support that New New York economist, Henry Roald. He argued that the drowning of the business sections of Manhattan was the watershed event for not just climate change, but also the economy. You don't think that Super Storm Sandy heralded the end of old New York?"

"No, Grandma," Duncan said through gritted teeth. "It was the sheer weight of all of the storms, floods, desert winds, frost on the orange groves. All the disasters, going on long after the country had spent the disaster relief funds. Hurricanes Maria, Florence and Michael, on and on." Duncan looked up to see a smile on Coli's face.

"Ready to defend your thesis yet?" she asked feigning innocence.

"Yes, I have it ready to share."

"Good," nodded Coli. "You need some exercise. Muscles …"

"Atrophy with too much time spent in VR. You've said that before, more than once." Duncan grimaced.

"Not often enough. I don't want to see you pooling your ambient power allotment with friends and then spending too much time in VR while your body just wastes away. I don't want you to be a VR addict."

"I wouldn't. You're exaggerating."

Coli looked Duncan in the eye. "I am not. Last night on the news you saw the Current Reality Emergency Crew cleaning out that apartment. You saw them bringing out the emaciated bodies and corpses. All those poor people who preferred Virtual Reality to real life."

"Some futurists think that moving into Virtual Reality and staying there is the next evolution for humanity."

"Well, we don't yet have the technology to do it. We still have bodies that need exercise, food, and friends in CR, so start moving." Coli caught her breath and thought for a bit. "In fact, go for a walk or bike ride. See if you can find your Grandpa Orlando while you're out. Don't forget your bike helmet." She leaned forward to give him a grandmotherly hug. "You are so cute. Just like your grandpas."

Oh, oh, thought Duncan. Here she comes, arms outstretched for love. He felt a little silly at his age but he reached down and hugged her.

"Hug, hug, hug. You sure do like to hug your family, Grandma. How come?"

"Just making up for lost time."

A Message from Katrina

Duncan bent down again and submitted to one more. He wondered when Coli would notice that he was too old to be hugged by his grandma. Probably never. For sure, not just yet!

His path led him through the kitchen where his mother was setting the table and his father stirring something on the electric stove. It smelled delicious. At least their own solar cells created enough power to keep the stove and freezer functioning. He said, "I'm looking for Grandpa."

"Good. Tell him it's supper," his mother replied. "He's probably up at the Point. He goes up there this time of year."

Duncan hurried down the stairs and walked through the Club. Raylene was already restocking the bar for the evening. Thelma and Burt, the cleaning crew were setting down the chairs on the clean floor. Rockin' Randy was already bent over the bar, nursing one more beer. Duncan felt sorry for the defeated old man. His diesel trucks became less and less popular as their buyers went to VR where they could posture and roar from any avatar and truck they wanted.

He had better say 'hi' to Randy. After all, 'bums on seats and beers in hand' had paid for his education.

"Hey, Randy. Where y'at?"

Randy turned in Duncan's direction with the glazed look of one in Virtual Reality. His winking WiFi earbuds came into view. Didn't he know that only young girls wore those? Randy blinked twice and entered Current Reality.

"How y'all, Duncan?"

"Finished my research project today, sir."

"That's good. You can get a real job, real soon." Randy smirked and turned back to his drink.

Duncan was reminded of why he didn't really like the guy.

Partway along the path to the Point, Duncan heard the soft strains of a familiar lament. Yes, there was Orlando, sitting on the bench and looking to the southwest where New Orleans used to be. He was softly singing part of *The New Earth Song*.

> "Hurricanes roared in to break them,
> Coastal cities, rich and proud.
> Shattered bits among the high tides,
> Was all the future, storms allowed.
>
> It's taken far too many a year,
> And far too many a tear,
> To conquer all our fear,
> And see the message clear.

A Message from Katrina

Our future can be bright
If we treat our planet right.
And we can carry on, can carry on
Yes, we can!"

"Grandpa, supper!"

"Heading back now," answered Orlando.

Duncan smiled by way of reply. He bet his grandpa was playing only for himself and not even sharing in VR. Old folks were pretty slow at using technology fully.

Orlando continued, "I was just thinking, remembering the way things used to be. When your great grandfather, Reverend Weekes, wanted to move his parishioners before Hurricane Katrina happened, people thought he was crazy. No one wanted to accept that climate change was real and that our coastal cities would be drowned."

"Yeah, you've mentioned that before, Grandpa", sighed Duncan, reminding himself that patience was supposed to be one of the virtues of being a farmer. He thought again about one of the restoration schemes found in the course of his research.

In 2007 there had been a plan, supposedly supported by the Army Corps of Engineers, to barricade the entire shoreline behind levees. Then they would pump the mud being washed down the Mr. Go Canal back into the marshes. After that they planned to dump sand to buttress the shrinking barrier islands. Opening a new section of the Gulf to gas and oil drilling would pay for the enormous cost of $500 million. It was all to have been completed by 2017. Looking back, Duncan found it amazing that people actually believed that gas and oil companies could, or would, fix the problems they were creating.

Even the massive 2010 oil spill from the offshore drilling rigs in the Gulf wasn't taken seriously. The destruction of shoreline and fish habitat went unreported at the time. He shook his head in amazement at the way his grandparents' generation just didn't get it. They refused to accept that capitalism by its very nature had to keep expanding, thus bringing about the Anthropocene that he and his generation now tried to live in.* He looked up from his musings in time to see his grandfather regarding him sadly.

"Hurricane Katrina was a message that most people didn't want to understand. Americans sent tax and relief money to rebuild. No one could accept the loss of New Orleans." Orlando's eyes clouded over as he remembered.

"Many people left after the first big storm. Many more didn't return when Rita pounded the city a month later. Reverend Weekes' parishioners, and Coli and I, left for something better. But too many were still there when

A Message from Katrina

Hurricanes Bert and Sally roared in. The city fell into more disrepair and despair as each storm came in."

Duncan slid off his bike and settled down on the bench beside his grandpa. "My research on Galveston showed that folks there, many employed in the oil refineries in the area, found it ever harder to hear the climate change message." He felt proud of all he knew about Galveston's demise. "They were pounded by Hurricane Rita, maybe worse than New Orleans in 2005. Then, Hurricane Ike roared in 2008, doing more damage. The next big hurricane was Harvey in 2017. It didn't just roar in. No way! Harvey gave devastating rain and flooding for more than a week. The destruction cost billions to repair. Some areas were never rebuilt."

Looking sad and old, Orlando shook his head. "Nobody wanted to believe the truth. We were just guzzling too much gas and oil. Burping and farting too much from all our machines into the atmosphere. Finally, in 2031, the truth could no longer be denied. We couldn't repair and rebuild our waterfront cities. Even our great ones."

Orlando sighed again as he looked off to where New Orleans had been. He couldn't see the waves washing against the ruins, but his mind's eye saw the drone footage after the last big storm. Waves sweeping against metal and cement wharfs and bridges. Tears shone in his eyes as he looked at Duncan. "New Orleans was the first of the sea coast cities to be declared Independent by the President. Galveston was the second."

"Independent!" sneered Duncan. "You know what that meant. No more FEMA or Red Cross aid or grant money. Nothing for anyone still there. No federal aid at all." He couldn't understand why his grandpa just accepted stuff like that.

"How else were they going to get the last people to leave? Common sense didn't seem to work and the resettlement money was rejected as not being enough. How long could the rest of America support settlements that just weren't sustainable? Isn't that what your analysis of the Agrarian Resettlement clearly shows—that resettlement of towns and farmlands creates a more sustainable lifestyle in Post-carbon America?" Orlando smiled at Duncan with satisfaction.

Duncan should have known better. Most of the time, his grandpa appeared to be what he was, a laid-back jazz musician. Only under great provocation, or the weight of memories, did he show that he listened to everybody and knew what was going on.

Orlando picked up his guitar and started the walk home. Softly, he sang the song to the end.

" Climate change affects us all,
Oh, send the message far and wide.
Local and sustainable we'll try,

A Message from Katrina

To combat climate change is why.
Our future can be bright,
If we treat our planet right.
And we can carry on, can carry on
Yes, we can!"

Jacqueline Swann

Notes

Author's Preface-*p6 'hieroglyphic stairway' from *Love Letter to the Milky Way*. 2011 by Drew Dellinger. Reprinted by permission of White Cloud Press

Chapter 1-* p11, *Macbeth*, Wm Shakespeare, Act1, Scene 7

Chapter 3-*p25, p28 much of Jordan Weekes presentation is based on the excellent description of south Louisiana and its people provided in *The Ravaging Tide* by Mike Tidwell.

Chapter 5-*p61, *Exodus,* Chapter 9, Verse1-Bible, King James, Electronic Text Centre, University of Virginia Library

Chapter 8-*p93, many of the details of the hurricane are based on information from *Hurricane Katrina, Time Books,* 2005

-*p96, *King Lear*, Wm Shakespeare, Act 1, Scene 4

Chapter 9-*p111, Many of the details of the hurricane were suggested from a photo account in *Hurricane Katrina*

A Message from Katrina

(Time Books). Some of the details were invented or used fictitiously by the author.

Chapter 18-*p211, The Road not Taken, *Mountain Interval*, 1916, Robert Frost

Chapter 19-*231, Richard Heinburg, <u>postcarbon.org</u>

-*p240, Transitions Towns Movement, <u>transitions.org</u>

-*p248, Dr. Elaine Ingham, Oregon State University, research and studies on aerated compost tea

Chapter 20-*p250, Wendell Berry, *Orion* magazine, Jan/Feb 2007

-*p253, Gayle Hudgens, *Collaborative Spunk*, 2002

-*p253, The Natural Step, <u>www.naturalstep.ca</u>

Chapter 21-*p259, Saudi saying from Richard Heinberg's *The Party's Over*, p81

-*p276, *Facing the Anthropocene*, fossil capitalism and the crisis of the earth system by Ian Angus

Jacqueline Swann

Works of Interest

Below is listed some of the sources which informed the author's imagination.

Angus, Ian. *facing the anthropocene*, fossil capitalism and the crisis of the earth system 2016

Barry, Wendell. *Orion* Magazine, 2007

Cline, Naomi, *This changes Everything* 2014

Dellinger, Drew, *love letter to the milky way,* White Cloud Press, 2002

Hurricane Katrina, Time Life Pictorial Essay 2006

Heinberg, Richard. *The Party's Over.* New Society Publishers, 2003

Hudgens, Alice Gayle. *Collaborative Spunk.* The Feisty Guide for Reviving People and Our Planet, SOS Press, 2002

Kingsolver, Barbara. *Animal, Vegetable, Miracle.* HarperCollins Publishers, 2007

Organic Gardening-oct/nov 2005

A Message from Katrina

Rubin, Jeff. *Why Your World Is About To Get A Whole Lot Smaller.* Random House Canada, 2009

Stella Natura. Camphill Village Kimberton Hills. Kimberton, PA, 2006

Tidwell, Mike. *Bayou Farewell.* Vintage Books. New York, 2003

Tidwell, Mike. *The Ravaging Tide.* Free Press, Simon and Schuster, Inc. 2007

Jacqueline Swann

The New Earth Song

by Jacqueline Swann

Chorus
It's taken far too many years,
And far too many tears,
To conquer all our fears,
And see the message clear.
Our future can be bright
If we treat our planet right.
And we can carry on, can carry on
Yes, we can!

1.Hurricanes roared in to break us,
Coastal cities, rich and proud.
Shattered bits among the high tides,
Was all the future, storms allowed.

(music)

2.And there upon the Great Plains,
Rivers ran thru city streets,
Houses drowned beneath the long rains,
Left the people stunned and meek.

(music)

3. Then the high winds hit the cities,
Left the people blind and cold,

A Message from Katrina

Shocked and silent in the darkness,
Like in storied days of old.

(music)

4.And the storm winds felled the giants,
Clear-cut acres with a gust,
Raining trees on trucks and houses,
Banks and people goin' bust.

Chorus
It's taken far too many years,
And far too many tears,
To conquer all our fears,
And see the message clear.
Our future can be bright
If we treat our planet right.
And we can carry on, can carry on
Yes, we can!

5.When the beetles mined the pine trees,
Summers went from dry to drier.
Leaving mountaintops of tinder,
Future fuel for storms of fire.

(music)

6.Flames screamed across the grass land,
Houses blossomed in a flash,
Leaving only fading memories
Buried deep within the ash.

(music)

7.When snow storms hit the orchards,
Oranges and lemons froze.

285

Many died in icy crashes,
And insurance costs, they rose.

(music)

    8.The tornado hit our new house,
Fifteen seconds changed our day,
Left our home as blasted litter,
And a mortgage still to pay.

    Chorus
Each crisis gives us pain,
But shows us lessons for our gain.
Our future can be bright
If we treat our planet right
And we can carry on, can carry on
Yes, we can!

    9.When the glaciers in the mountains,
Flowed their melted waters low,
Left the highlands dry and thirsty,
And the flooded fields below.

(music)

    10.Now, none of us is watching,
As the Arctic glaciers swelter.
Ocean levels swamp our cities,
As our trade and commerce falter.

(Altered final chorus… change of key and/or melody … may
be repeated for emphasis)

A Message from Katrina

Climate change affects us all,
Oh, send the message far and wide.
Local and sustainable we'll try,
To combat climate change is why.
Our future can be bright,
If we treat our planet right.
And we can carry on, can carry on
 Yes, we can!

Jacqueline Swann

ACKNOWLEDGMENTS

Thank you to Peggy Hess, Janice Nairne, Claire Rudd and Mary Rudd, for their reading of the first draft, their editing and encouragement. Thank you to the members of Book Chat—Wynne DeMonye, Sharron Harper, Judith Hutchison, Shirley Prince, and Bonnie Ruttan who came month after month to help with the last drafts. Their line by line editing and suggestions for changes in the larger questions of character descriptions and motivations kept me working on the book.

Thank you to David Lord for extensive editing and helping me navigate the self publishing universe.

Thank you to Dianne Cheetham for helping me write and print the music for my song. I could not have done that without her assistance. Many thanks to Dianne Dvorak who played and sang the original version of The New Earth Song.

ABOUT THE AUTHOR

Jacqueline Swann is a retired teacher. During the course of her career she taught mostly English and French to students aged from four to sixty-four. In the mid-1970's Jacqueline and her husband, Gary, went 'back to the land' and started an organic farm and eco-forest near Port Alberni. This post-industrial seaport is located at the head of a long inlet in the middle of Vancouver Island, British Columbia, Canada. There they raised three children. Two grandsons visit the farm often. Gary and Jacqueline have recently added biodynamic methods to their farming.

During these years of work, work, work Jacqueline did indulge in some leisure time. She has always been an avid reader. Hurricane Katrina inspired her to write as well. This story has evolved with the long term assistance and persistence of family and friends. She thanks them all.

She has always understood how planet Earth nurtures and confines us. She knows that if nothing else does, our own self-interest should propel us to nurture our planet.

Made in the USA
Middletown, DE
22 April 2019